If und

consid

There was no fumbling, no awkwardness. Philip kissed each inch of flesh he bared until Holly tingled all over.

"You take my breath away, Holly. You're so beautiful."

And she believed him, or at least believed that to *him* she was. The way he gazed at her made her feel more beautiful and desirable than she had ever thought possible.

"You're an absolute delight," he said, pulling her down beside him.

Delight. That was what they gave each other. Their caresses were playful and erotic, demanding yet gentle.

Philip took his sweet time with her. He wanted Holly to trust him completely, to give herself completely. He absolutely refused to believe that she was incapable of ever feeling love and joy again. He would prove her wrong. Maybe not now, not tonight, but eventually...

Dear Reader,

Welcome to the Silhouette **Special Edition** experience! With your search for consistently satisfying reading in mind, every month the authors and editors of Silhouette **Special Edition** aim to offer you a stimulating blend of deep emotions and high romance.

The name Silhouette **Special Edition** and the distinctive arch on the cover represent a commitment—a commitment to bring you six sensitive, substantial novels each month. In the pages of a Silhouette **Special Edition**, compelling true-to-life characters face riveting emotional issues—and come out winners. Both celebrated authors and newcomers to the series strive for depth and dimension, vividness and warmth, in writing these stories of living and loving in today's world.

The result, we hope, is romance you can believe in. Deeply emotional, richly romantic, infinitely rewarding—that's the Silhouette **Special Edition** experience. Come share it with us—six times a month!

From all the authors and editors of Silhouette **Special Edition**,

Best wishes,

Leslie Kazanjian,
Senior Editor

BEVLYN MARSHALL

Goddess of Joy

Silhouette Special Edition

Published by Silhouette Books New York

America's Publisher of Contemporary Romance

SILHOUETTE BOOKS
300 East 42nd St., New York, N.Y. 10017

ISBN: 0-373-09562-7

First Silhouette Books printing Novcmber 1989

Printed in the U.S.A.

Books by Bevlyn Marshall

Silhouette Special Edition

Lonely at the Top #407
The Pride of His Life #441
Grady's Lady #506
Radio Daze #544
Goddess of Joy #562

BEVLYN MARSHALL,

a Connecticut resident, has had a varied career in fashion, public relations and marketing, but finds writing the most challenging and satisfying occupation. When she's not at her typewriter, she enjoys tennis, needlepoint, long walks with her husband and toy spaniel, and reading. She believes that people who read are rarely bored or lonely because "the private pleasure of a good book is one of life's most rewarding pastimes."

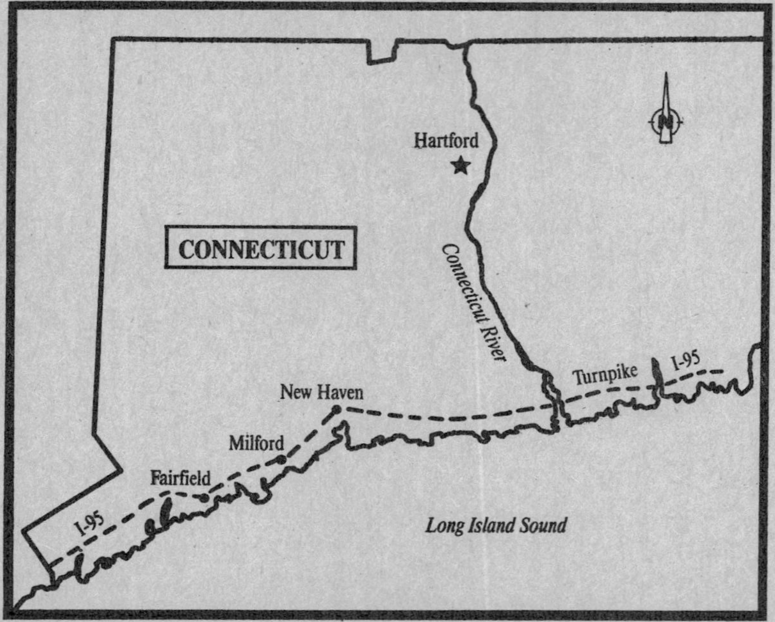
CONNECTICUT
Hartford
Connecticut River
Turnpike
I-95
New Haven
Milford
Fairfield
I-95
Long Island Sound

Chapter One

I'll get out here and walk the rest of the way, Jack," Philip Irons told his driver when the car became trapped in New Haven traffic. He didn't want to be late for an important dinner with potential investors in his next building project.

"Do you want me to wait in front of the restaurant for you, Mr. Irons?"

"No. Just show up there at ten. Go have dinner yourself in the meantime. On me." He handed the chauffeur fifty dollars, then swung open the back door and got out.

Twilight was blending into night, and although it was officially spring, there was a harsh winter chill in the air. Philip shoved his hands into the pockets of his pin-striped suit jacket, ruining the elegant lines of it, and remembered a poem he'd read long ago about April being the cruelest month. Something about the stirring of memory and desire. In his youth he'd been a voracious reader, but he hadn't picked up a book in years. This thought depressed him as he hurried down the block. There never seemed to be time for the simple pleasures of life anymore.

He passed an antique shop and automatically paused to take in the dimly lit window display. The one interest Philip retained from his younger days was his fascination with miniature Japanese carvings called netsuke. Through the years he'd acquired a museum-quality collection of them and was always on the lookout for another to add to it. His sharp eyes slid past a pewter teapot, an ugly kerosene parlor lamp, an even uglier portrait of somebody's double-chinned ancestor, a china figurine of a terrier and an assorted collection of tarnished silver candlesticks. Nothing here for me, he quickly decided.

But his attention was pulled to the Staffordshire dog. There was something right behind it... Philip tilted his head. A two-inch netsuke was barely discernible in the shadows. His pulse jumped. It was his long-lost Goddess of Joy. He had never forgotten her. He had always regretted giving her up. And there she was, coyly hiding behind the china dog.

Hot tears sprang to Philip's eyes. He quickly blinked them away, embarrassed by his own sentimentality. But he couldn't help it. He hadn't seen his goddess for more than twenty years, and she was as beautiful as he remembered. Her beauty was impervious to age. She had been intricately carved in ivory more than a hundred years ago and would always remain perfect.

A sign declaring that the shop was closed hung in the window, but Philip pounded on the locked door with the frail hope that the proprietor might still be in back somewhere. He got no response. A knot of frustration tightened in his chest. What he wanted more than anything at that moment was to hold the goddess in his hand once again, to wrap his fingers tightly around her and never let her go. He actually considered ramming his shoulder against the door and breaking in to get her. He stifled this impulse immediately, amazed that he'd considered such a foolhardy action for even a second. He released a sharp laugh. Perhaps he hadn't changed so much through the years after all. He noted the shop's business hours posted on the door and resolved to come back first thing the next morning to claim his netsuke. He reluctantly turned and continued on his way to the restaurant.

Holly Murphey took a seat at the counter of Dino's Diner. She ate breakfast there every morning before going to Jerome Academy for Young Ladies, where she taught English. The glum waitress, after giving her a curt nod in greeting, poured her a cup of coffee.

"The usual, honey?"

"Yes, Gladys. The usual, please." Holly had discovered the great comfort of established habits since moving to New Haven four years ago.

"May I join you, Mrs. Murphey?"

Holly swiveled and smiled at the dapper old man standing by the vacant stool beside hers. "Please do, Mr. Brakenbiddle." How many times had they gone through this formal little ritual? she wondered. Hundreds. Like her, Mr. Brakenbiddle was a creature of habit.

"You look very pretty this morning," he said as he sat down. "Your gray sweater brings out the lovely blue of your eyes."

"Why, thank you, Mr. Brakenbiddle." How kind he was, Holly thought, always managing to find something nice to say about her appearance. "And I like your new bow tie."

The old man touched the bright red silk at his neck. "The devil made me buy it. You don't think it's too... wild, do you?"

Holly smiled. "Why not be a little wild once in a while? Especially on such a glorious day."

"Yes, it is glorious," Mr. Brakenbiddle agreed. "It's hard to believe that it was so chilly just last night. I took a stroll after closing up the shop, and the wind cut right through me. But today is absolutely balmy."

Gladys came back with Holly's toast and scrambled egg, slammed the plate down in front of her and glared at Mr. Brakenbiddle. "The usual for you, too, I suppose, Pops? A bran muffin and tea?"

"You're a genius, Lady Gladys," he told her.

"Yeah, it takes a real genius to remember what you two order every single day of the year." She snorted and left them.

Mr. Brakenbiddle shook his silver head. "Gladys seems to think we're in a rut, Holly."

"I suppose we are," she easily agreed.

"Well, it's not as bad for me, dear. I'm an old widower set in my ways."

"And I'm a widow set in hers."

"It's not the same thing at all!" Mr. Brakenbiddle protested. "You, Holly Murphey, are still a young woman with a long life ahead of you."

Holly sipped her coffee and said nothing for a moment. Four years ago she'd thought her life was over. Since then she'd passed through many stages of grief, from denial to rage to acute depression, and now she had finally accepted her loss. To reach this stage had been a long, painful process, and she wasn't quite ready to go on to the next one. Whatever that might be. Although she was slowly healing, she feared rushing the process. Her spirit yearned to be optimistic about the future, but the past shadowed her view of it.

"No one is guaranteed a *long* life, Mr. Brakenbiddle," she finally replied.

He reached out and patted her hand. "All the more reason to make the best of every day, my dear."

Gladys returned to fill Holly's cup, and Mr. Brakenbiddle clicked his tongue. "Don't encourage her, Gladys. She drinks far too much coffee as it is." He made the same comment every workday morning.

"I've been cutting down lately," Holly told him. "And I've been sleeping much better." Dreaming less about Daniel and Danny, she added silently.

"It shows," the old man said. "You really do look quite lovely today, despite that dowdy sweater you're wearing."

"Why, you just complimented me on it," Holly reminded him, not looking the least bit offended. She didn't give a hoot about clothes.

"No, dear. It was your eyes I was complimenting. That sweater is as drab as the rest of your wardrobe, I'm afraid. You should go buy yourself some pretty new clothes in bright colors to celebrate spring, Holly."

She shook her head. He was a sweet old man but a bit of a buttinsky. Still, she knew he meant well. "I'll let you be the fashion plate around here, Mr. Brakenbiddle," she said, straightening his new bow tie. "I have better ways to spend my hard-earned money, as you well know. By the way, has anything new come into your shop since my last visit?"

"Yes, a few choice items." He dunked his tea bag in the cup of hot water exactly five times and removed it. Holly would have been amazed if he'd dunked it fewer or more times.

"Well, do tell," she urged him. Through her friendship with Mr. Brakenbiddle she'd become interested in collecting antique decorative objects. It was her chief pleasure and indulgence. Not that she could afford to indulge herself too often. But now and then she would buy herself a Victorian paperweight, or bisque statuette, or Limoges porcelain box—small treasures that gave her great satisfaction.

"I've acquired a Staffordshire mantel dog that's quite nice," he said. "I've put a two-hundred-dollar price tag on it, but you, Holly, could have it for less if it captures your fancy."

"I'll stop by to take a look at it after my last class today," she said. "Around four."

"Oh, I'll have closed shop by then. I have a doctor's appointment."

Holly's eyes filled with concern. "Are you ill?"

"No, no. I'm perfectly fine, dear." He cut his bran muffin into four sections and slowly buttered each one.

"Then why are you going to the doctor if you're perfectly fine?" Holly persisted, alarm ringing in her voice. "You're keeping something back from me."

"Good heavens! Don't jump to such terrible conclusions. I'm only going for my annual checkup," Mr. Brakenbiddle said a bit impatiently. "I'm as fit as a fiddle, so there's no need for such trepidation."

"Sorry I overreacted." Holly smiled sheepishly. "But I care about you."

"And I care very much about you," Mr. Brakenbiddle said in a gentler tone. "I didn't mean to sound impatient with you, my dear. I understand why you tend to react that way at times."

He was the only close friend Holly had made in New Haven since she'd started a new life for herself there, the only one she'd confided in completely. She got along well with the other teachers at the academy, but mostly she kept to herself. Rather, she kept her past to herself. The staff and students knew that she'd lost her husband in an accident before moving to the city, but she'd never been able to bring herself to tell anyone but Mr. Brakenbiddle that she'd lost her son, too. She couldn't bear to utter the boy's name aloud although he remained as much a part of her as her very heartbeat.

Gladys slapped Holly's check on the counter. "Have a nice day," she commanded. "You, too, Pops," she said, slapping down Mr. Brakenbiddle's. She turned away abruptly and hurried to the kitchen.

"How I wish Gladys would smile, just once, when she said that," Mr. Brakenbiddle stated wistfully. After he'd consumed his muffin and tea he waited politely, hands folded on the counter, for Holly to finish her breakfast.

"Shall we walk to the corner together?" he asked when she had.

Holly nodded. It was part of their ritual. Mr. Brakenbiddle took out a leather change purse and extracted a shiny dime from it, which he left as a tip. As he slowly made his way to the cash register Holly placed her own tip on the counter then stealthily added two quarters to his. She did this every morning because she knew Mr. Brakenbiddle had a generous nature and didn't mean to be cheap. He was just behind the times when it came to tipping. Besides, Gladys was grouchy enough in the morning!

She slipped on her navy jacket, gathered up her lesson notebook and purse and joined Mr. Brakenbiddle at the cash register. He took her arm after they left the diner, and they strolled down the block.

"Look!" he said as they passed a bucket of bright yellow bouquets outside a florist's shop. "My wife, bless her soul, called them daffy-dillies. Let me buy you a bunch, Holly."

"How sweet of you," she said. She didn't take the same pleasure she once had in flowers, but she sensed his need to give them to her as a tribute to his wife's memory.

Mr. Brakenbiddle purchased the daffodils, presented them to Holly with a little bow, and they continued on their way.

"Why don't you come to the shop right now and take a look at that Staffordshire dog?" the old man suggested when they paused at the corner where they usually parted.

Holly agreed. She really wasn't interested in mantel dogs but decided to keep Mr. Brakenbiddle company while he opened up his shop. He seemed especially lonely to her this morning. It occurred to Holly that perhaps it was *she* who was more lonely than usual on this warm, sunny day. She watched a laughing young couple dash across the street holding hands, and her heart squeezed tight. She and Daniel used to always run together hand in hand, laughing.

"Well, here we are," Mr. Brakenbiddle said, stopping before his shop door. He took out his keys. "The dog is in the window. Do you like it?"

"It's charming," Holly said. But she felt no desire to possess it. The morning sun made everything in the window glow, and she noticed a small ivory figure behind the dog. "What's that?" she asked, pointing to it.

"Ah, the netsuke!"

"Netsky?" she repeated. "That sounds Russian, but it looks so Japanese."

"It is, my dear. *Ne* means root in Japanese, and *tsuke* to fasten. Pronounced net-skee." He unlocked the door and ushered her in. "Would you like to take a closer look at this one?"

"Yes, please." She very much wanted to hold the tiny figure.

Mr. Brakenbiddle carefully took it out of the window and placed it in her waiting palm.

"Oh, how beautiful she is!" Holly exclaimed.

"Indeed. She's called the Goddess of Joy."

Holly gazed at the smile of rapture on the figure's face. "Perfect," she said.

"Yes, perfect craftsmanship," Mr. Brakenbiddle agreed. "Notice how beautifully the folds in her kimono are carved. Such a graceful pose, don't you think?" He tilted his head to the side and clasped his hands to his chest, duplicating it.

Holly couldn't help but laugh.

"What a nice sound that is," the old man said. "I rarely hear you laugh, Holly."

"I must be under the influence of the Goddess of Joy," she joked. She turned the netsuke in her hand, carefully studying each detail. "What are these two tiny holes at the base for?" she asked.

"Well, I'll tell you." Mr. Brakenbiddle beamed at the opportunity to show off his expertise. "You realize that the traditional Japanese kimono has no pockets, don't you?"

Holly had never given it much thought, but she nodded to encourage him to continue.

"So where could the fine Japanese gentleman of yesteryear store the little necessities of life, such as money or medicine or tobacco?"

"Or the fine lady her lipstick and comb?" Holly kidded him.

"Actually, it was only the men who had need for netsuke. Until recently Japanese women rarely left the house and had no reason to carry personal equipment around."

"But I still don't understand how a tiny figure like this could help anybody carry anything."

"Ah, I was getting to that, my dear. The men carried their essential items in lacquered boxes called inro. Now the inro was attached to a cord, which passed through the kimono's wide sash."

"Called the obi," Holly volunteered.

Mr. Brakenbiddle nodded. "Correct. And the netsuke was attached to the *other* end of the cord and thrust between the obi and kimono from the top, leaving the inro to hang free. The netsuke was used as a toggle of sorts."

"A toggle? What a prosaic description of something as exquisite as this." Holly stroked the figure in her palm with her finger.

"Well, the purpose of netsuke, don't forget, was utilitarian. Originally they were simply pieces of root or bamboo. Artisans eventually recognized the decorative possibilities, and netsuke developed into intricate carvings in wood, jade and ivory. The one you're holding is attributed to Hojitsu, one of the finest craftsmen in Edo during the nineteenth century. He was acclaimed for his depiction of realistic, sensitive faces."

"She does look very real to me," Holly said. "So alive! I must have her, Mr. Brakenbiddle."

He shook his head. "I hope your heart isn't set on it, my dear, because the price is rather steep. I'm selling the netsuke on consignment, so I can't negotiate, I'm sorry to say."

Holly closed her fingers around the ivory figure. "How much?"

The old man sighed. "A thousand dollars."

That was far too much to spend on a whim, Holly thought as her heart plunged. It seemed all joy was beyond her limits now. She was about to hand the netsuke to Mr. Brakenbiddle, but something deep within her protested. She couldn't let go of it, even though it would make a big dent in her savings account. There was something about the goddess's jubilant expression that reminded her of...her former self.

"I'll write you out a check, Mr. Brakenbiddle."

He looked stunned. "Are you sure you can afford it, Holly?"

"I'm sure I *can't*! But don't worry. My check won't bounce. I'm going straight to the bank after I leave here to transfer the money."

"I'm not the least concerned about that," the old man said in an injured tone. "What does concern me is that you're making such a hasty decision, which isn't at all like you, Holly. You're usually so prudent."

"Not today, I'm not. And I blame it on the goddess." She placed her notebook and bouquet on his oak counter, which was piled high with books and papers, and took her checkbook from her purse.

"Here's what I'm going to do for you, Holly," the old man said. "I'll forgo my ten-percent commission on the sale and charge you—"

"Absolutely not!" she interrupted vehemently. "You have a business to run, Mr. Brakenbiddle." She hurriedly made out the check and handed it to him. "I haven't felt so good in a long time."

He chuckled softly. "It seems the goddess's joy is rubbing off on you, my dear."

"If that's the case, then she's worth ten times the amount I paid." Holly tucked the netsuke in her jacket pocket, picked up her bouquet and blew a kiss to the elderly dealer before she headed out the door. There was a spring in her step as she hurried to the bank down the street, and the people she passed on the way smiled at her.

As his car passed by, Philip spotted a pretty woman in a dark blue jacket waiting to cross the street. He noticed her because she was clutching a bunch of daffodils. The moment she was out of view he forgot about her. His only interest at the moment was getting his precious goddess. Impatient as always, he told his driver to let him out in front of the antique shop and circle around the block until he found a parking space.

When he glanced in the window, cold apprehension inched up his spine. He threw open the door and marched into the shop. "Where's the netsuke?" he demanded.

Startled, the elderly shopkeeper almost dropped the feather duster he was carefully flicking over a Tiffany lamp. He gave Philip a wary look. "I beg your pardon, sir?"

Philip took a deep, calming breath. He supposed he did look like something of a hoodlum, dressed in his faded jeans and a black sweatshirt. "Excuse me. I didn't mean to be so abrupt. I'm inquiring about the ivory netsuke that was in the window. I saw it last night and made sure to get here the moment you opened for business. I want to buy it."

"Sorry, but I just sold it to my friend Mrs. Murphey. I opened the shop early for her."

"What? You sold my goddess?" Philip shouted.

The old man backed away from him and went behind the counter, as if to put a protective barrier between them. "Yours, sir? Are you claiming it was stolen property?"

"No, not at all." Philip cautioned himself to keep a cool head. "At one time I owned that particular netsuke, but then I traded it for something else. Now I want it back."

"Well, I'm very sorry to disappoint you. But it seems the Goddess of Joy has eluded you."

"Oh, no, she hasn't." Philip's smile was tight. "Tell me how to get in contact with this Mrs. Murphey, and I'll buy it back from her. It's as simple as that."

"Not so simple. She may not want to part with it."

"Not even if I offer her double the amount she just paid for it?"

The dealer sniffed to show disbelief. "You'd be willing to give her two thousand dollars?"

"Absolutely," Philip said without blinking.

At that the gent raised a hand to his throat and played with his bow tie for a moment. "Who are you, sir? A dealer?"

"No, no. I'm just a private collector," Philip replied irritably. He always tried to be direct and honest with people but that often seemed to complicate matters rather than simplify them. He took a card from his wallet and handed it to the old man. "I'm in the construction business."

"Irons Building and Development, Incorporated. Fairfield, Connecticut. Philip Irons, President."

"Yeah, that's what it said the last time I looked at it, too."

The old man gave him a slow once-over, his eyes pausing at the hole in the sleeve of the sweatshirt and the patch on the leg of the jeans. "You certainly don't look like any president of any corporation to *me*, Mr. Irons."

Philip maintained his equanimity with a great effort of will. "Listen, buddy, I didn't come in here for the third degree. All I want is that netsuke. Why are you making this so difficult?"

"Because I'm beginning to think that I underestimated its value, and my name is Mr. Brakenbiddle, if you please."

"No, you didn't underestimate its value." Philip leaned against the counter and looked at him earnestly. "It's an unsigned Hojitsu, and your lady friend paid fair market price for it. But it's worth more to me for sentimental reasons."

"Hm." Mr. Brakenbiddle fiddled with his tie again. "I don't want my friend to be bamboozled."

Wondering how he could convince the old man that he was being straight with him, Philip lowered his head and rubbed his tense neck. His eyes fell upon a notebook on the cluttered countertop. The name written in the upper corner of it immediately caught his attention—Mrs. Holly Murphey. And beneath it, written in the same prim handwriting—Jerome Academy for Young Ladies. He raised his head and kept his expression as blank as when he played poker with his construction crew.

"I'm not out to bamboozle anyone," he told the dealer.

Mr. Brakenbiddle shook his head. "I'll have to get back to you, Mr. Irons."

Philip nodded. "You do that. You have my card." He left the shop without another word.

His car was double-parked outside, and Philip hopped in the back.

"All set to go to the construction site now, Mr. Irons?" the driver asked.

"Not yet, Jack. This is going to take a little longer than I originally planned. Next stop is Jerome Academy for Young Ladies. Ask that policeman at the corner where it is." Philip wished that he had worn a suit and tie to make a good impression on Mrs. Murphey. He pictured her as elderly and refined and only hoped she wasn't a stubborn old goat like her gentleman friend, the antique dealer.

Holly watched her students straggle into the classroom. They varied in shape and size, nationality and race, but they had one thing in common. They were all teenage girls. And Holly knew it would be difficult to keep their attention on this glorious day.

She recalled how hard it had been for her to concentrate on her studies when she was their age and spring was in the air. Her life had seemed spread out before her like a lush, green lawn in those days. It hadn't been so very long ago, after all, but Holly still found it hard to believe that she'd once been so confident that the future would bring her only good things. She would never regain that carefree optimism. The loss of it had been too traumatic. But at least she was now able to accept and enjoy the small pleasures of life. That was enough for her. That was more than she'd expected last year at this time.

She smiled down at the netsuke in her hand, then put it in the pocket of her navy pleated skirt. She opened the window to let in the warm breeze, checked the clock on the wall and decided it was time to settle down her students—or at least attempt to.

"A gaggle of giggling girls!" she called out as they took their seats with much shuffling, tittering and murmuring. "What's that called, class?"

"An insult, Mrs. Murphey?"

Holly smiled. "No, Melissa. At least I didn't intend it as such. But let's try this one. A league of ladies with lilting laughter. Yes, that's much better." She was winging it because she'd forgotten her lesson plan notebook at the antique shop. "What's the repetition of initial sounds in adjacent words called? We went over this yesterday."

"Alliteration," her best student, Jade, volunteered.

"That's right. And now I'd like you to give me some examples of alliteration, class. I'll give you five minutes to jot down a sentence. Try to be as creative as possible."

Melissa raised her hand. "First I have a question, Mrs. Murphey. Who gave you that bunch of daffodils on your desk?"

"A dear friend of mine."

"A *male* friend?"

Holly sighed with exasperation. She was well aware that her students felt sorry for her, widowed so young, and were constantly trying to put some romance into her life. "Why must a friend be qualified by gender?" she asked. "Will someone please give me a definition of gender?"

"Sex!" a voice in the back row squealed. And that word alone was enough to make the whole class explode with merriment.

Yes, spring had certainly arrived, Holly thought, smiling indulgently. "You now have *four* minutes to complete your assignment," she said.

She turned her back to them, picked up a stick of chalk and began writing a poem about spring on the blackboard. It was one that meant a great deal to her and could still pierce her heart with pain. But it was the only one she could call up from memory, without her notes.

Holly was printing the last line when she heard a hiss of whispers behind her. She swiveled to face her class but was met by the backs of their heads, a sea of waves, curls and crimps in various hues. Her students were all looking toward the back of the room, where a tall man leaned against the open doorway, arms folded across the expanse of his black sweatshirt. Holly's immediate thought was that he was a student's impudent boyfriend. But then she realized that, despite his youthful attire and body, he was closer to her age.

"May I help you?" she asked sharply.

"I hope you can, Miss. I'm looking for Mrs. Murphey."

His reply generated a few giggles.

"*She's* Mrs. Murphey, mon," Jade said in her Jamaican accent, ready as always to supply the correct answer.

"Oh, I'm sorry." Philip crossed the room feeling more self-conscious than he had in years. "I thought you were another student, Mrs. Murphey."

More giggles.

But Holly's expression wasn't the least bit amused. Her face drained of color as memories clawed at her brain, tearing through the present and bringing the past into sharp, searing focus. She had opened the door of her home to a man dressed in dark colors on a sunny winter day four years ago. *I'm looking for Mrs. Murphey, Ma'am,* he'd said. She had smiled at him, a little confused. Why would a policeman be looking for *her*?

"What do you want?" she demanded from the man standing in her classroom now.

They certainly weren't used to male visitors at Jerome Academy for Young Ladies, Philip surmised as he took in her shocked expression. He dared a glance at the rapt audience of students and shifted uncomfortably. "Actually, it's a private matter," he said in a hushed tone. "Could we step outside to discuss it, Mrs. Murphey?"

Oh, no, Holly thought. Something awful has happened. Again! She was sure this man brought bad news about someone close to her. She nodded and led him to the hall.

"Tell me," she said in a low, even voice. "Tell me straight out and get it over with quickly."

The young policeman had beat around the bush. *There's been an accident, Mrs. Murphey.* Oh, dear. On this street? *No, Ma'am. On the lake.* The lake? But that's where my husband and boy are. *They were both rushed to the hospital.* Then they're going to be all right, aren't they? The policeman had averted his eyes. *No, Mrs. Murphey. They aren't.*

As she waited for the stranger in black to speak, Holly replayed the conversation that burned forever in her memory.

What an intense, impatient woman, Philip thought as he studied Mrs. Murphey for a moment. She'd looked so young from across the room but now, close up, she seemed to age before his very eyes. Her own eyes were the most vivid blue he'd ever encountered, but perhaps they looked so bright because her face was so pale. Even her lips were colorless. Her dark brown hair was like a sleek battle helmet around her white face, just covering her ears and forming a widow's peak at the top of her high forehead. Her dark eyebrows were harsh slashes. Her features were pleasant enough, but the severity of her expression vanquished her natural prettiness.

"You look like you're about to give me a detention slip, Mrs. Murphey," he said, trying to relax her with a mild joke.

It didn't work. "Tell me why you're here," she demanded again.

Philip decided that all attempts at humor would be futile and got right to the point. "I've come to inquire about the netsuke you purchased this morning."

"The netsuke? That's why you're here?" Relief flooded through Holly, and she pressed her hand to her chest. She could feel the pounding of her heart slow down immediately.

"Yes. I want to buy it back from you."

Holly raised her chin and glared at him. Although she realized that he hadn't intentionally frightened her by appearing in her classroom so unexpectedly, her initial impression of him remained tainted. How dare he barge into her life and demand that she sell him her treasure? She had taken an immediate dislike to him. His stance, his direct gaze, his easy, anticipatory smile all demonstrated to her that he was a man used to getting what he wanted.

"I have no intention of selling my goddess, Mister..."

"Irons. Philip Irons." He put out his hand.

Holly stared at it but made no move to accept it. She hoped her deliberate rudeness would hasten his departure.

It had just the opposite effect, though. He shifted in place, as if digging the rubber-soled heels of his boots into the tile floor. His lips stretched into a wider smile, forming parentheses around his mouth. Holly guessed he was in his late thirties. Yet there was something inherently boyish about him. Perhaps it was his ruddy complexion. Or his thick russet hair, crisp with vitality. He had a golden aura around him that didn't suit his surname. His eyes did, though, Holly observed. They were a hard, piercing, metallic gray. Philip Irons was a man of steel, she concluded. But he couldn't make the slightest dent in her.

"I'm sure I can convince you otherwise, Mrs. Murphey," he said. "I'll pay you two thousand dollars for the netsuke."

She was taken aback for a moment. "That much?"

Philip licked his lips, tasting victory. He'd learned through the years that he could buy anything he wanted for the right price. Almost anything, anyway. "What would you prefer? A check or cash?"

Holly shook her head. "Neither. No, thank you, Mr. Irons." She slid her hand into the pocket of her skirt, touching the ivory figure with her fingertips. It gave her comfort. "I'm not interested."

He laughed sharply. "You're not interested in making a thousand-dollar profit in less than an hour? Come on, Mrs. Murphey. I don't have all day."

His presumptuousness offended her. "And I don't have a minute more to spare. I have a class to conduct, and I didn't appreciate your interrupting it. Goodbye, Mr. Irons." With that she left him standing in the hall and returned to her students.

Chapter Two

"I assume everyone has her sentence demonstrating alliteration completed by now," Holly said as she took her place in front of the class.

"Who was that guy, Mrs. Murphey?" bold Melissa inquired.

"Nobody important," Holly replied and continued without missing a beat. "Let's hear your sentence, Angelica."

The girl dutifully stood, flicked back her long hair and cleared her throat. "A magnificent man meandered into our room to meet with melodious Mrs. Murphey."

The class roared with appreciation. Holly joined in. Her students never failed to surprise and entertain her. She encouraged them to be outspoken. They were all scholarship students, some of the brightest girls in the city. She praised Angelica's use of alliteration without commenting on the subject matter and asked Melissa to read her sentence next.

She eagerly sprang up from her seat. "A handsome hunk hovered in the hall, heart hammering."

The class laughed again, but this time their teacher was not so amused. "I think I've heard enough examples to guess what the rest will be about," Holly said. "So let's turn our attention to a higher level of creativity, shall we?"

But before Holly turned to the blackboard she stole a glance toward the open doorway to assure herself that no handsome hunk still hovered in the hall. The hall was empty. Satisfied that Mr. Irons had departed, she breathed a sigh of relief. It was a very long, deep sigh.

"All right, class," she continued in a no-nonsense voice, pushing Philip Irons out of her thoughts. "I've written some lines from a Shakespeare sonnet on the board. I'll read them to you, and then we'll interpret their meaning."

"Why should we have to interpret them?" Melissa asked. "Shakespeare wrote in English. Either we understand what he said or we don't."

"Do you completely understand a person you just met, Melissa?"

"Well, no, but people are complicated."

"Yes, they are. And so is good poetry. You have to slowly peel away the layers before you get to the core. You have to be open-minded and patient, just as you would be during the process of making an acquaintance a true friend."

"Yeah, but making a good friend is worth the trouble," Melissa rebutted.

"Why?" Holly asked her.

"Because friends are *fun*," she answered. "And they feel sorry for you when you feel bad."

"So they're a pleasure and a comfort, right?"

"Yeah, right, Mrs. Murphey."

"Well, so is poetry, Melissa. Just give it a chance."

Holly turned to the board and read the first line. "'From you have I been absent in the spring.'" Her voice cracked. She took a deep breath and continued. "'When proud-pied April, dress'd in all his trim, Hath put a spirit of youth in everything.'"

There! She'd gotten through it. She'd sent those lines to Daniel during his first year away at college. How she'd pined for him! They'd grown up together and never been separated before. She'd joined him at the college the following year, and they'd taken a solemn vow never to be separated again.

Philip, pacing the hall out of view but within earshot, listened to Mrs. Murphey recite the poem, and the sadness in her voice assuaged his angry impatience with her. What caused it? he wondered. He'd noticed it in her eyes, too. What would make a beautiful young woman so sad?

It occurred to him then that she really was quite beautiful, in a subtle sort of way. Philip was usually attracted to women who advertised their good looks, but Holly Murphey seemed determined to camouflage hers. Why else would she wear such a god-awful sweater and dark, bulky skirt? But those eyes of hers—

Philip stopped his pacing and pulled himself up short. What the hell was he doing, dwelling on Holly Murphey's eyes? He didn't mess around with married women. Mrs. Murphey's thick wedding band hadn't escaped his notice, and the only interest he had in her was the Goddess of Joy she now had in her possession. *His* goddess.

He went to her classroom as soon as she'd dismissed her students. He wanted to settle his business with her quickly and get out of her life. The glacial stare she greeted him with didn't faze him one bit. "Okay, two thousand five hundred," he said without preliminaries.

"Please leave, Mr. Irons. We don't like strangers loitering around the academy."

He sighed with resignation. She obviously needed a little more time to consider his offer, and he had no choice but to give it to her. "I'll be happy to leave if you agree to discuss this further over lunch, Mrs. Murphey."

"There's nothing to discuss! I don't want to sell my netsuke. It's as simple as that."

"Chinese?" Philip asked as if she hadn't spoken. "Do you like Chinese? Or maybe Italian? Or Mexican? Hey, whatever you choose. You're calling the shots, lady." He'd let her think she was, anyway.

What would it take to get rid of this man? Holly wondered. A bulldozer? Her second-period students were straggling into the room, giving him curious looks. The girls from her first class were still hanging around the hall, waiting to see what would develop.

The last thing Holly wanted was rumors about her and a man in a black sweatshirt to start circulating around the academy. Didn't Philip Irons appreciate what an impact he was making on a school full of impressionable teenage girls? Most likely he did, Holly decided. He knew exactly what he was doing.

She lowered her voice. "There's a restaurant up the street called Dino's Diner. That's where I usually eat. I'll meet you there at noon. Now please leave."

"Bring the goddess," he told her. Then he walked out, whistling, as many pairs of eyes followed his departure.

"Nice butt," Holly overheard one girl whisper to another. She rolled her eyes. They would be whispering about Philip Irons's visit to her classroom for the rest of the week, she was sure.

Holly spotted him half a block away, waiting for her outside the diner. His height and build made him an easy man to recognize. Without realizing it, she quickened her step.

And without realizing it, Philip smiled when he saw her coming. He liked the way her hair bounced around her pale oval face as she strode toward him. She was carrying a bulky navy jacket in her arms, and Philip realized that she was the woman he'd seen that morning, holding a bunch of daffodils as she waited to cross the street. No doubt she had just left the antique shop with his goddess. If only he'd arrived ten minutes earlier, he would have beaten her to it. But Philip wasn't one to rail against fate. He'd always rolled with life's punches and come out a winner. He gave Mrs. Murphey a confident wave.

"I'm sorry I'm late. Why didn't you wait inside for me?" she asked when she reached him.

"I'd rather wait outside on a day like today. Or any day, for that matter."

He looked like a man who spent most of his time outdoors, Holly thought. His face was weathered and tan. So were his hands. She noticed he was holding a brown paper bag. "What's that?" she asked.

"Lunch," he replied. "The diner was so stuffy and crowded that I ordered take-out. Ham and cheese and roast beef with mayo." He took her arm. "Come on. We'll have a picnic in the park."

Holly didn't budge. "Maybe I don't like that plan, Mr. Irons."

He released her arm and looked genuinely surprised. "What? You don't like ham or roast beef? No problem. We'll order something else for you."

"I happen to like them both, but that's not the point. What I *don't* like is being manipulated by you. You may have harassed me into meeting you here, but you're not going to drag me off on a picnic now."

"Hey, I didn't have anything devious in mind. I just thought it would be more pleasant." He shrugged. "Forget it. We'll eat in the diner."

The moment he acquiesced, Holly regretted voicing her objection. She didn't want to have lunch in a stuffy, crowded diner on such a delightful spring day any more than he did. "Oh, let's go to the green," she said. "Since you already bought the sandwiches." She started walking up the street.

He caught up with her in two long strides. "Are you always this contrary, Mrs. Murphey?"

"No. But I find you extremely irritating, Mr. Irons," she answered honestly.

He laughed as if she'd just paid him a charming compliment. "All I've done is offer you a lot of money. What's so irritating about that?"

"You won't take no for an answer."

"It's not my favorite word," Philip admitted. "But I hardly think that I'm harassing you, Mrs. Murphey. Okay, I admit that I'm a little persistent but—"

"A little? Ha!"

"Listen, that netsuke means a lot to me."

"To me, too."

"It couldn't possibly mean as much to you, dammit!" Philip grabbed her arm as she started to cross the street and pulled her to the curb.

Holly jerked from his grasp. "I don't appreciate being manhandled, Mr. Irons."

"Sorry. But the traffic light just changed. I didn't want you to get run over."

"Oh. Thank you."

"Don't mention it."

They waited for the light to change again in silence, then crossed the busy intersection and headed toward the New Haven Green.

"Why does the netsuke mean so much to you?" Holly asked when they reached the park.

"It's a long story. Why should you care?"

His rebuff set her teeth on edge. "I don't."

"Then why ask?"

"I'm sorry I did."

They turned away from each other and looked around the crowded park. All the benches around them were occupied.

"Let's forget about lunch. There's no place to sit," Holly said.

"Sure there is. What about that bench in the sun? The one with the boy dressed in leather sleeping on it."

"What do you propose we do? Sit on top of him?"

Philip ignored her sarcasm. "Wait here. I know just the magic words to make him disappear."

Holly watched as he leaned over the boy and spoke to him. The boy got up immediately, looking absolutely delighted at being disturbed. Holly understood why he appeared so affable when Philip took out his wallet and handed him some money. The boy went on his merry way.

"Okay, we got us a reserved seat," Philip called, beckoning her to join him.

She approached, shaking her head. "Money talks," she said dryly.

"The trick is to get people to listen," he replied. "Sit down, Mrs. Murphey. We'll have ourselves a cozy little chat in the sun."

She placed her coat between them and perched on the bench. "I stopped by the antique shop before meeting you," she told him.

"Yeah, I figured you would." He took out the two sandwiches. "Ham or beef?"

"Ham." He gave it to her and she placed it on her lap but made no move to unwrap it. "You *figured* I would?"

"Of course. That's why you stalled me this morning, isn't it? You wanted to talk to the old man first. How much did he advise you to hold out for?" Philip took a big bite of his sandwich.

Holly almost wished that he would choke on it. "The only reason I went to see Mr. Brakenbiddle was to find out how you tracked me down. I knew that he would be far too discreet to tell a complete stranger where I worked."

"He didn't. You left a school notebook on the counter."

"Congratulations on your sneaky bit of detective work, Mr. Irons."

"Hey, there was nothing sneaky about it. That notebook was right out in the open."

"What if it hadn't been?"

Philip shrugged. "I would have had no choice but to wait until Brakenbiddle contacted me."

"That's exactly what you should have done instead of barging into my classroom this morning."

Philip took a can of cola from the bag and snapped it open. "I never wait around when I don't have to, Mrs. Murphey. Here." He handed her the soda. "And I prefer to deal directly with the person I'm doing business with, not go through some middleman."

"But we're not doing any business together, Mr. Irons. As difficult as this may be for you to fathom, I didn't purchase the netsuke to make a quick profit. I have no intention of ever parting with the Goddess of Joy."

His wide mouth twisted into a smile of disbelief as he snapped open another can of soda. "Not until you hear the right numbers, anyway. Just tell me the top price you and Brakenbiddle came up with. I'll either accept it or dicker you down a few notches."

Holly tossed back her head, and her glossy cap of dark hair shimmered in the sun. "I'm not going to *dicker* with you." Her straight little nose twitched as she stressed the word with distaste.

Philip raised his eyebrows in admiration. Mrs. Murphey was a lot tougher than she looked. He was more inclined to admire than resent her for holding out on him, though. She knew she had something he wanted, so why shouldn't she try to get as much as she could for it? Her pal the antique dealer had probably run a credit check on him. He ate in silence, considering the situation.

Holly unwrapped her sandwich and nibbled at it, at the same time observing the man beside her with quick, sidelong glances. The sunlight shot fiery glints through his dark russet hair as the breeze ruffled it. It would be soft to the touch, Holly knew. But the profile beneath the thick, wavy thatch was blunt, unyielding.

He finished his sandwich and took a long swig of his cola, throwing back his head. Holly noted his strong jaw line and the muscular cords of his neck. She knew, from the business card that Mr. Brakenbiddle had given her, that Philip Irons owned some sort of construction company. That fit with his physique. Even before she'd known Irons's occupation, she'd imagined him in a showdown with a bulldozer. She could easily picture him the winner of such a confrontation. But she wasn't going to let him bulldoze her. She brushed her hand against her skirt pocket and felt the Goddess of Joy there, safe and secure.

Philip noticed her movement out of the corner of his eye. "You have the goddess in your pocket, don't you?" he asked softly.

She considered lying to him but couldn't. She nodded without looking at him.

"Would you let me hold it for just a moment?"

Holly hesitated, reluctant to hand it over to him.

"Please," he added.

She turned to face him and saw such longing in his expression that she relented. She slowly pulled the ivory figure out of her pocket.

Philip took it from her without a word and cupped it in his large palm, studying it intensely. How small it was. What delicate perfection. It had been years since he'd held it like this. He recalled the first time. His palm had been callused in those days. He'd gone to a flea market looking for carpentry tools and paused at a table cluttered with junk. Spotting the netsuke, he'd picked it up out of idle curiosity. He'd never seen one before and had no idea what it was. But the fine craftsmanship had impressed him. The exquisite beauty of the piece had touched his soul. It still did.

Observing how Philip's strong, stubborn features had softened as he gazed at the goddess, Holly felt a stab of compassion for him. He seemed so vulnerable at that moment. Her heart opened to him. But then he folded his long, strong fingers around the delicate ivory figure in a possessive grip. "Five thousand," he said. "And that's my final offer."

Holly's heart closed tight again. "Please give her back to me, Mr. Irons."

Her? So Mrs. Murphey personalized the netsuke, too, Philip thought. This surprised him. He looked deeply into her eyes and could see no avarice in them. Perhaps she wasn't holding out for more money, after all. If that were true, then how would he get through to her? What else could he possibly offer her?

Holly's open hand remained empty as she waited for him to return the Goddess of Joy. She stared at him, and the steely gray of his eyes melded with the clear blue of hers. "Give her to me," she whispered.

Philip dropped the little figure into her waiting palm.

Holly could feel the heat of his own hand on it. She slipped it into her pocket. "I'm sorry," she said and meant it.

"*You're* sorry!" Philip's laugh was hollow. He shook his head. "Why does the goddess mean so damn much to you, Mrs. Murphey? It's only been in your possession for a few hours."

"It's a long story. Why should you care?" she replied, repeating his words.

"Touché." He touched the left side of his chest. "Well, it seems we've reached an impasse here. I want to buy, but you don't want to sell."

"That sums it up in a nutshell, Mr. Irons." She was relieved that he'd finally accepted the situation.

"Then there's no sense bashing my head against a brick wall, is there?" He stood abruptly.

Holly's relief washed away in a flood of unexpected disappointment. Philip Irons was about to walk out of her life as suddenly as he'd come into it. "Goodbye," she said, offering her hand. "Thank you for lunch."

Her small hand disappeared into his big one as he shook it. "You hardly ate any of yours," he said. He held her hand a moment longer than necessary before releasing it. "I want you to know that I offered you a fair price for the netsuke, Mrs. Murphey. More than fair. If you don't believe me, you can check it out with a few dealers who know the market. I'm sure they'll confirm that my offer was more than generous."

"I believe you."

"Good." He smiled tensely. "Are you going to tell your husband that you turned down a four-thousand-dollar profit today?"

"My husband is dead, Mr. Irons."

"Oh." He sat beside her again without even thinking about it. "That's too bad. I'm sorry."

Holly had heard those words a thousand times before and nodded wearily. She hoped he wouldn't question her about it, as people often did in an effort to be sympathetic. She'd learned to deflect their interest by asking them a personal question first. "What about you, Mr. Irons? Are you married?"

"No. I've been divorced for years."

Holly's heart quickened, but her expression remained bland as she tore off a piece of crust from her sandwich and tossed it toward a waiting pigeon. Both she and Philip watched the bird peck at it for a moment as if it were the most fascinating thing they'd ever witnessed.

"You're a good teacher," Philip finally said. "I can only base my opinion on what I overheard in the hall, but you seem to really enjoy your work."

His comments warmed Holly to the tips of her toes. "I do. The students at Jerome are very special."

"And very privileged, I suppose, going to a fancy private school for young ladies."

"Just the opposite," Holly told him. "The academy was founded by Isabel Jerome at the turn of the century to give underprivileged girls a chance to further their education. She left a huge endowment to insure the school's continuation."

"I didn't see one male in the place."

"That was the major stipulation in Isabel Jerome's will, I'm afraid. All students *and* teachers must be female. That's why you caused quite a stir this morning, Mr. Irons."

"Was that the only reason?"

"That and your exceptional good looks, of course," Holly replied seriously.

"Oh, I doubt it."

"No need for false modesty, Mr. Irons. You were fishing for a compliment, and I gave you a sincere one."

He looked startled for a moment, then smiled. "Maybe I *was* fishing. You're the most self-contained woman I've ever met, and I wanted some kind of personal response from you before we parted."

Holly looked away from him. Ever since she'd laid eyes on Philip Irons, she'd been responding to him on a highly personal level and doing her best to hide it. She hadn't responded to a man so forcefully for years, and it upset her equilibrium. She threw another piece of crust to the bird.

Philip glanced at his watch and stood reluctantly. "I'm late for an appointment. I hadn't planned on staying in New Haven this long." He paused. "Or leaving empty-handed. Take good care of the goddess, Mrs. Murphey. You're her guardian now. I'll keep in touch with you."

"Why? I'm not going to change my mind."

"Yeah, but I've just made up mine."

Her pulse jumped again. "What's that supposed to mean?"

"You'll find out."

He gave her a parting smile, then turned and walked away. Holly observed how his black shirt emphasized his wide shoulders and broad back, how his jeans accented his long legs and narrow hips. His masculine symmetry struck a vibrant chord in her, one she'd been deaf to since she'd lost her husband. After Philip disappeared from view, she leaned against the bench and closed her eyes, letting the sun caress her face. His image remained vivid in her mind's eye. Would he really keep in touch? she wondered. Her eyes flew open. Of course he would. She was the goddess's *guardian*. He hadn't really accepted her refusal to sell it to him. He'd just changed his tactics.

Chapter Three

So, Holly, I'm dying to know," Mr. Brakenbiddle said first thing the next morning when he joined her for breakfast at the diner. "What happened between you and that Irons fellow yesterday?"

"Nothing happened. He offered me more money for the goddess, and I refused."

Mr. Brakenbiddle stopped dunking his tea bag. "How much, if I may ask?"

Holly saw no reason to keep it from him. "Five thousand dollars."

"That much! That's way over market value, Holly. I called a few experts in the field yesterday afternoon, and they confirmed my initial assessment of the piece. I was greatly relieved, let me tell you. I would hate to think I undervalued a piece I took on consignment."

"But what if you hadn't opened the shop early for me, Mr. Brakenbiddle? Would you have sold the goddess to Philip Irons for much more?"

"No, my dear. The price had been set at a thousand dollars. I would have sold it to him for that amount, too."

"That makes me feel a lot better," Holly said.

"It couldn't have worked out better as far as I'm concerned," Mr. Brakenbiddle assured her. "You were *meant* to have the Goddess of Joy, my dear. It's going to bring you good fortune." He leaned closer to Holly. "I also made a few calls about Irons yesterday. He's a wealthy man, I discovered, one of the biggest condominium developers in Connecticut."

"I didn't ask you to check him out," Holly said sternly. "I wish you hadn't."

"It's always wise to know who you're negotiating with, my dear."

She shook her head. "I'm not negotiating with Mr. Irons. Don't you understand, Mr. Brakenbiddle? I want to keep the goddess."

"I appreciate how attached you are to it, Holly." The old man divided his muffin into quarters. "But in my business, I see people part with treasures they hold dear all the time when they need extra money."

"But I don't *need* extra money. What would I do with it? Go on a vacation all by myself?"

"Why not? Who knows who you'd meet."

"I went on one of those cruises for singles," Gladys said, apparently overhearing their conversation as she passed by. "And all I met was a bunch of creeps."

After divulging that nugget of information, she continued on her way to the other end of the counter.

"You can always count on our charming waitress to add a note of cheer," Mr. Brakenbiddle murmured. "But getting back to this Irons fellow, Holly. Avid collectors like him don't give up easily. Mark my words, you'll be hearing from him again."

Holly not only marked his words, but took them to heart. A guarded heart.

That afternoon Holly stood in front of her class explaining structural grammar to her restless students. She found the lesson as boring as they did but tried not to let on. It was the last period of the day, when even the most motivated student had trouble concentrating. The girls' interest perked up considerably, though, when a young man carrying a big white box sauntered into the room.

"School supplies should be delivered to Ms. Salverone in the front office," Holly informed him.

"This ain't school supplies. My instructions were to go directly to Mrs. Murphey's classroom. Are you her?"

Holly refrained from correcting his grammar and nodded.

He plunked the box on her desk. "Enjoy!" he said before leaving.

Holly suspiciously eyed the glossy box, imprinted with the name of an expensive French bakery.

"Aren't you going to open it?" a student inquired.

Holly slowly lifted the lid and smiled at the sight of a plump array of sugar-dusted cream puffs and chocolate-covered eclairs nestled in frilly doily beds. "Oh, dear," she said. "I think I've just opened Pandora's box, girls, and released thousands of calories upon us. Help yourselves!"

They didn't need to be asked twice and shot out of their seats to crowd around her desk.

"Bliss," one girl moaned, sinking her teeth into a pale golden pastry.

"Who sent us this special treat, Mrs. Murphey?" another asked through a mouthful of custard.

"There's no card in the box," Holly replied evasively. She had a pretty good idea who had, though.

So did one of her students. "It must have been that guy Melissa told us about yesterday. The one who crashed Mrs. Murphey's first-period class."

"You're jumping to conclusions, Shirley," Holly said.

"Well, so is everybody else," the girl testified in her own defense. "*Everybody's* talking about him, Mrs. Murphey." She licked some chocolate off of her fingers. "Wait until they hear about this."

"Maybe you *are* jumping to conclusions, Shirley," someone else commented. "Didn't Melissa say that this guy mistakened Mrs. Murphey for a student at first?"

"Mistook," Holly automatically corrected.

"Right. Which proves that he didn't even know her when he walked in. So why would a complete stranger be sending her gifts?"

"Ever hear of love at first sight?" Shirley asked, helping herself to another pastry. "He sees her across a crowded room, and his heart stands still."

Holly laughed. "Really, Shirley. I think you've been reading too many romances. Mr. Irons came to see me on personal business, that's all. If his heart had stood still, he'd be dead now. But I'm happy to report that he was in fine health the last time I saw him."

"Aha!" one of the girls cried out. "We know his last name now."

"We know even more than that." Shirley smiled slyly. "Our teacher just gave away that she's familiar with the state of Mr. Irons's health because she saw him again." She turned to Holly. "And when was that, Mrs. Murphey? Last night over a cozy candlelit dinner for two?"

"Brilliant deduction, Shirley *Holmes*!" someone said.

The few girls who weren't holding pastries applauded. The others nodded enthusiastically in agreement.

Holly threw up her hands. "I give up! You're all impossible." She was grateful that the bell rang then, putting an end to their playful inquisition. "Class dismissed. Please feel free to take more pastries before you leave."

"But you haven't had one yet, Mrs. Murphey," Shirley pointed out.

"They say love makes you lose your appetite," another girl said so wistfully that everyone giggled.

Holly picked up an eclair. "Share the rest, girls." She handed the box to one of them.

They left the classroom, chattering and laughing. As soon as they were gone Holly tossed the doily-wrapped eclair in the wastebasket. In fact she hadn't had much of an appetite for the last day or so. She blamed it on the sudden change in the weather. Spring always affected her metabolism.

She sat at her desk and reviewed her lesson plans for the next day. She could hear the echo of quick footsteps in the hall. Teachers and students were hurrying home. Holly had no reason to hurry home. There was no one waiting for her there. She took the netsuke from her pocket and placed it on the desk to keep her company.

"I know what he's up to. He's trying to butter me up to get to you," Holly told the tiny ivory figure.

The Goddess of Joy smiled at her.

"I'm not going to fall for such an obvious ploy, though," Holly continued. "I'm glad he didn't leave a note in the box. Now I don't have to call and thank him."

The goddess only smiled more.

That evening Holly made herself a light salad for dinner. The goddess joined her at the table, right between the salt and pepper shakers. Holly usually ate dinner alone and rarely went out in the evening. Lately, though, she'd been considering enrolling in one of the many continuing educational programs offered in New Haven.

Perhaps a bonsai workshop, she thought as she picked at her salad and perused a brochure from the Edgerton Garden Center Club. The netsuke had sparked her interest in all Japanese artforms. She'd known, from the moment she'd first seen the figure, that it would somehow change her life. No, that wasn't quite right, she thought. Her desire to get on with her life had been slowly building for months, and the goddess's joyful smile had only strengthened it.

Holly wasn't superstitious about the figure, but she was growing more and more fond of it. She'd never bought herself anything that had given her such satisfaction or pleasure. It irritated her that Philip Irons had offered her so much money for the goddess. It made her uncomfortable to own something so valuable. Of course, it was only worth that much to *him*. Why?

She picked up the goddess and cradled it in her palm, recalling how longingly Philip had gazed at it. "Why does he care so much about you?" she asked aloud.

And as if in response to her question, the phone rang.

"Hello, Mrs. Murphey," Philip said when she answered. "How are you?"

She immediately recognized his voice, and the sound of it warmed her. But she kept her own voice cool. "Actually, I'm a little annoyed, Mr. Irons," she replied.

"Not with me, I hope."

"Yes, with you. I wish you hadn't sent those pastries to the academy today. It's not that they weren't appreciated. My students gobbled them up. But now they're assuming all sorts of things about you and me."

Philip chuckled. "Like what?"

"That you have a personal interest in me."

"Then they're right. I do. I'd like to get to know you better, Holly."

It was the first time he'd called her by her first name, and it sent an unexpected shiver through her. She gripped the receiver more tightly. "Unlike my students, I'm not an impressionable teenager, Mr. Irons. It's the goddess you're interested in, not me."

"Why should one interest discount the other?" he asked. And while she was trying to come up with a logical reply, he sprang another question on her. "What are you doing tomorrow evening?"

"Nothing," she answered automatically, since that's what she usually did on Saturday night.

"What a coincidence! Neither am I. Why don't we have dinner together?"

"No. I don't think that's such a good idea."

"I think it's a great idea, Holly. So here's the plan. I'll pick you up around seven and—"

"I said no, Mr. Irons. This new approach of yours isn't going to work. Gifts and dinners aren't going to help you get the goddess."

He didn't say anything for a moment. Holly thought that it would be the perfect time to hang up, but somehow she just couldn't bring herself to do it.

"Listen, something's been bothering me for a couple of days," he finally said. "And I think you can help me out."

"What is it?" she asked despite her better judgment.

"A poem that's been nagging at my brain."

"A poem?" She had to hand it to him. He was full of surprises.

"Yeah, this poem about April that I read long ago. That it's the cruelest month of the year. Do you know it?"

"It's from *The Waste Land*, by T.S. Eliot."

"Recite it for me, will you?" he asked softly.

How Holly wished she could at that moment! "I'm sorry, Philip. I don't know it by heart. It's too long, anyway. And I haven't read Eliot since college days. But if I remember correctly, he says that April is cruel because the spring rain stirs the dull roots of memory with desire, making us long for what we can no longer have. At least that's my interpretation."

"Do you long for what you can no longer have, Holly?"

His question was so direct that she answered it with the same directness. "Yes. But not as much as I used to."

"Well, I know a poem that's not very deep but a lot more cheerful," he said. "April showers bring May flowers."

She laughed. "Do you always look on the bright side of things, Mr. Irons?"

"You bet. And you just called me Philip a minute ago. I prefer that. Now about dinner Saturday night. Do you like lasagna?"

"Don't you ever give up?"

"Didn't I overhear you tell your students to be open-minded, Holly? Yet here you are shutting me out. You asked them to give poetry a chance. Why don't you give *me* a chance?"

His voice was so persuasive that she was on the edge of accepting his invitation. And then Philip pushed her over the edge.

"If you have dinner with me I'll show you my netsuke collection," he said. "I have another Hojitsu goddess even more beautiful than yours."

"Ha! I doubt it, Philip."

"I'll prove it to you. We'll have dinner at my place. Tell me what time you'd like me to pick you up."

"I'd prefer driving there myself." She couldn't believe she was giving in to him with only this small stipulation. She tried telling herself it was because she wanted to see his Hojitsu. And she did. But she had to admit to herself that she wanted to see him again, too. Very much.

He began insisting that he come to New Haven to get her, but she held firm about that at least. So he quit arguing while he was ahead and gave her directions to his home. "You'll see a sign for Green Meadows on your left," he concluded. "Just tell the guard at the gate house that I'm expecting you. He'll direct you from there."

"To what? Your castle?" she joked.

"Well, yeah. Isn't every man's home his castle?"

"I'll be there around seven," she said.

And the moment she hung up, she regretted accepting his invitation. She would call him back and call it off immediately. No. That would make her appear ridiculous. She would wait until tomorrow and call to say something had come up and she couldn't make their date. It wouldn't be lying exactly. Something *had* come up—all her fears and misgivings.

* * *

Holly drove down I-95 Saturday evening with a mixture of anticipation and dread playing havoc with her stomach. She was actually going through with it!

What was the big deal anyway? she asked herself, tightening her grip on the steering wheel and gritting her teeth as she passed a big truck. She could handle herself with Philip Irons. He didn't intimidate her in the least. In fact, he was rather... nice. No, that was far too mild a word for him. Personable? That wasn't quite right, either. Holly slowed down and took the Fairfield exit. Sexy? Provocative? Exciting? She took a sharp right. She hadn't thought of a man in those terms for a very long time.

She followed the directions Philip had given her and soon spotted the sign for Green Meadows. She pulled up to the gate house and waited for the guard to emerge. She felt a little out of her element. She'd never visited anyone with a home security system more sophisticated than a barking dog. A smiling man came out. It was Philip.

He opened the passenger door and climbed into her car. "I figured you'd be right on time or not show at all," he said.

The vague scent of his clean, sharp after-shave appealed to Holly. "Don't tell me you moonlight as a security guard."

He laughed. "I got restless waiting at the house for you, so I strolled down to the gate to meet you." He waved to the man silhouetted in the small building, and the iron gates opened. "Go straight up the hill," he told Holly. "And watch out for the speed bumps."

She gave him a sideways glance as she followed his directions. His white dress shirt stood out in the twilight. Dark tie. Dark jacket. She was glad she had worn the silk navy dress she usually reserved for formal school functions.

She looked at the road and noticed condominium units to the left and right, almost invisible behind the shield of manicured hedges. "Oh, for goodness sake!" she said, smiling. "I'd assumed Green Meadows was your private estate, Philip."

"Disappointed?"

"No, relieved!"

"This is one of my most successful condominium projects," he said. "It's a prime piece of real estate, and when it came on the market fifteen years ago I risked everything to get it. The property used to belong to a railroad tycoon."

Holly continued driving up the hill very slowly because of the bumps in the narrow, winding road. She rounded a bend, then she saw it at the very crest of the hill—a stone mansion complete with a looming tower.

"Oh, no, Philip. Say it isn't so."

"But it is so, Holly. That's my home sweet home. I figured that if it was good enough for a railroad baron, it was good enough for me."

"But it's so..." She bit her bottom lip.

"Ostentatious?" he supplied enthusiastically. He laughed when she didn't deny it.

The white stones paving the circular driveway crunched beneath the car wheels. They stopped in front of a wide flight of marble steps leading to the arched entrance. Philip got out and hurried to open

Holly's door. He took her arm and led her up the steps. When they reached the massive carved door Holly looked back at her little economy car. It seemed so out of place in this grandiose setting. She felt out of place herself.

"You're not thinking of leaving already?" Philip asked, noticing her glance at her car. She could feel his fingers tighten around her arm slightly.

"Are you kidding?" she said. "Not until I get the grand tour, mister. I've never been inside a mansion before."

Philip gave her a boyish grin. "Neither had I until I bought this one. Come on. I'll show you around my humble abode."

The entrance hall had a flagstone floor, high, molded ceiling and marble columns. "This foyer alone is bigger than my entire apartment," Holly said. Her voice sounded hollow in the vast expanse.

"You don't think it's quite right for one person to live in a house this size, do you, Holly?"

She shrugged. "If you want to flaunt your wealth it's none of my business, Philip." She grimaced as she heard the words come out of her mouth. They sounded more critical and disapproving than she'd intended.

But Philip didn't seem to mind in the least. "You hit the nail right on the head, lady! I live here because in my business you've got to show off your success. I'm in constant need of backers for new projects, and nobody wants to put money on a loser. I use this house as a showplace, and it's also my corporate headquarters. The whole east wing is offices, with a cafeteria, gymnasium and day nursery for my employees."

Holly couldn't decide if he sounded like a caring employer or a feudal lord of the manor. She would have to learn more about Philip Irons before coming to any conclusions about him. The only thing she knew for sure was that he fascinated her.

"What about the west wing?" she asked.

"Come see," he said, taking her hand.

Holly allowed her small palm to nestle against his large, warm one as he led her across the vast entrance hall and into a room even bigger. "The living room," he announced, then laughed. "Excuse me. The *drawing* room, as the decorator insisted on calling it."

Decorated it certainly was, Holly observed—with elaborate tables and chairs, overstuffed sofas upholstered in chintz, yards of embroidered material draping the tall windows, expensive handwoven rugs on the parquet floor. Almost every inch of wall space was covered with mirrors and paintings. Every table surface was crowded with expensive art objects. It made her a little dizzy to take it all in.

"Impressive," she managed to say.

"Yeah, it sure as hell is, isn't it?" Philip squeezed her hand and winked.

They continued hand in hand, through the salon (decorated in purple brocade, which Philip said he couldn't stand), the music room (where Philip played "Chopsticks" for her on the grand piano), the library (the leather-bound sets of books on the shelves, Philip said, were in foreign languages he couldn't read), the prim, ruffled "informal" sitting room (where Philip confessed he'd never actually sat and wouldn't if his life depended on it), then the dining room.

Holly tensed. The long table was set for twenty, with crystal wineglasses, gold-rimmed china and silver candelabra.

"I assumed we would be having dinner alone, Philip," she said, dismayed.

Her dress was all wrong for an elaborate dinner party. More importantly, she'd been looking forward to sharing a quiet meal with Philip. She'd found herself liking him more and more as they passed through each elaborately decorated room because of his self-effacing and droll comments during the tour.

"Oh, we're not going to eat in this mausoleum," Philip said, waving his long arm to encompass the giltwood console tables and mirrors, and imposing marble busts and cut-glass chandelier. "The table's set for tomorrow night. A little dinner for some of my dearest friends." His tone was ironic.

They went to the drawing room and Philip offered Holly a drink.

"Sherry, please," she said, although she was really dying for a cup of black coffee.

He poured a glass for each of them from a decanter on one of the side tables.

"Darn, I thought you were going to ring for the butler," Holly said, pretending disappointment.

"Naw, that's not my style. I can't stand having people at my beck and call. A cleaning service comes in twice a week, and I hire a caterer when I entertain. I can manage just fine on my own day to day."

"A simple man with simple needs," Holly said, tongue in cheek, as she roamed around the sumptuous room, sipping her drink.

"That's me all right," he agreed, watching her, a little smile on his face.

"You haven't showed me your netsuke collection yet," Holly reminded him.

"I will in good time."

She met his eyes across the room. Even at a distance she could see the steely sparkle in them. "Now's as good a time as any," she said.

"First we'll have dinner. And if you're very good and eat all your vegetables, that'll be your reward."

Was he patronizing her? Holly wondered. Humoring her? Yet his robust, open features disarmed her. When he crossed the room to take her hand again she didn't object.

"Where are we going now?" she asked.

"My place." He grinned at her confusion. "My *real* home. The rooms you've seen so far are just for show. I spend most of my time in the tower. That's the next stop on the tour."

They left their barely touched glasses of sherry on a marble-topped table, crossed the vast foyer, then turned down a narrow, dimly lit hall that ran along the back of the house. It was too narrow for the two of them to walk abreast, and Philip released her hand to lead the way.

"Is this a secret passageway?" Holly joked to cover up her nervousness.

"Not secret but definitely off-limits."

His reply did little to assuage her uneasiness. "Why do I get the feeling I just stepped into a Gothic novel?"

He chuckled. "Don't worry, Holly. There's no insane Mrs. Rochester locked away in my tower."

"No mad Mrs. Irons, either, I assume."

She noticed Philip's broad back stiffen. But he replied in a bantering tone. "My ex-wife may have driven others crazy, but she was perfectly sane herself. She flew the coop long ago."

Had he bought and refurbished this mansion for his wife? Holly wondered. And why had she flown the coop?

Philip stopped so suddenly that she smacked right into his solid back. Hard. She practically ricocheted off of it.

"Oops, sorry." He quickly turned and grabbed her shoulders to steady her. "Are you all right? I almost knocked you out."

"I almost knocked myself out, you mean. I wasn't paying attention to where I was going."

"But it was all my fault. You had no idea we'd reached the end of the hall." He kept his hands on her shoulders and scrutinized her face, concerned. "You could have broken your nose!"

She wriggled it a few times. "Nope. It just got mashed a little. It's fine."

"That's a relief. Because it's such an adorable nose." Then he lowered his head and kissed the tip of it so lightly that Holly wasn't quite sure he had. He released her and opened a heavy door at the end of the passageway. "Still game to climb up to my tower?"

Holly hesitated for only an instant. "I haven't come this far to turn back now."

Why did she trust this man so much? she asked herself. He'd given her absolutely no reason to. No reason *not* to, either. The little kiss on the nose had been too brief, too comforting to be considered a pass. What bothered Holly most was that she had found such comfort in it.

He flicked a light switch that illuminated a stone staircase. "It would be more dramatic if I used a candle to light the way, I suppose."

"I prefer electricity," Holly assured him. She looked up at the winding staircase. The steps were steep. "This tower isn't haunted, is it?"

"Not that I've noticed."

"No bats flying around the belfry, I hope."

"No bats. No ghosts. No vampires. No mice, even." He paused. "But I guess I should warn you about King Kong."

Holly laughed. "King Kong is your roommate?"

Philip nodded and gave out an exaggerated sigh. "He can be a little difficult to live with. He tends to get overly excited at times. Especially when he sees a beautiful woman. So beware."

Holly let the flattery lap over her like a delicious wave. "Forewarned is forearmed. Lead on, Philip! I'll face the mighty Kong and stare him down."

"No! Whatever you do, Holly, don't look at him! He'll be all over you if you do."

"But you'll protect me, won't you?"

"All I can promise, fair lady, is that I'll do my manly best against the beast." Apparently Philip thought that such a dramatic statement called for another kiss. This time he kissed her on the cheek, again as lightly as a brush of butterfly wings.

And again Holly didn't object. She followed him up the stairs with buoyant anticipation.

There was another door at the top of the landing. The iron hinges squeaked when Philip opened it. Holly peeked inside and saw nothing but darkness.

"Is he in there?" she whispered, enjoying the little joke.

"We'll know in a minute, won't we?" Placing his hand on the small of her back, Philip gave Holly a gentle push over the threshold, then touched a wall switch that turned on all the lamps.

Holly had a moment or so to take in a large room, with its simple furnishings, white stucco walls and dramatic Gothic windows. And then a blur of fur came bounding toward her, yelping with hysterical glee.

"Halt, King!" Philip commanded.

But Holly welcomed the beast like a long-lost friend.

Chapter Four

It's okay, Philip, I'm crazy about dogs," Holly said, allowing King Kong to nuzzle against her as she scratched his back.

"Even this one?" he asked, amazed.

Holly smiled down at the dog, a mutt of such mixed breeding that he was a unique species unto himself. King had a thick, motley coat in hues that ranged from tan to black, floppy ears, a long whip of a tail, a square muzzle, and languishing hazel eyes that pleaded for love and attention.

"Especially this one," Holly said, letting the creature lick her hand with mighty swipes of his tongue. "He looks like a cartoon composite of a dog. I wouldn't be surprised if he started speaking to me." She crouched to be at eye level with King. "What's up,

Doc?" she asked in a fairly good imitation of Bugs Bunny. The dog gazed at her, puzzled.

"Good try, Holly," Philip said. "But the King speaks only to me. We have fascinating philosophical discussions when we're alone."

She straightened and looked him in the eye. "You're not putting me on by any chance?"

Philip pretended shock at such an accusation. "I would never, ever lie to you, Holly Murphey. Would I, King?"

The dog leaped up on him, and Philip gave him a hearty hug as Holly looked around the tower room. She decided it suited Philip much more than the sumptuous showplace below. The arched windows were undraped, a few thick sheepskin rugs were scattered over the expanse of wide-planked floor, and plain pine bookshelves, packed with mostly paperbacks, lined the walls. There was a kitchen area in one corner and a few chairs and sofas grouped around a stone fireplace in the other. A circular wrought-iron stairway led up to... Philip's bedroom, no doubt.

"Well?" he asked her. "What do you think?"

"I like it," she replied. "No gilt, no chintz, no brocade, no ruffles."

"No interior decorator," Philip added. "King wouldn't allow one to set foot in here. The dog has excellent taste, but he sheds like crazy." Philip brushed some dog hairs off his black jacket and gray pants, then turned his attention to Holly and began brushing hairs off the front of her skirt.

A blush rose to her cheeks as his hand roamed over the silk fabric, molding the shape of her thighs. "I think you got them all off, Philip," she said, stepping back. "Thank you."

"My pleasure," he said, a smile tugging his wide mouth.

She turned away from him, hoping her high color would recede before he noticed. She felt foolish, blushing like a schoolgirl when all he had done was brush dog hairs off her skirt. Still, his touch had been more like a caress. Or had that been her imagination?

"So where's this famous netsuke collection of yours?" she asked.

"Upstairs in my bedroom."

"Oh, really?" Holly attempted an expression of haughty sophistication but couldn't quite carry it off. Her wariness must have shown on her face because Philip looked amused.

"Yes, really," he replied. "And I assure you that I didn't move my collection up there to seduce you tonight, Holly. If I kept the display case down here, King would be sure to knock it down."

"Well, let's go take a look," she said, hoping her no-nonsense demeanor would demonstrate to him that seduction was the last thing on her mind.

"After dinner," Philip said. "I don't know about you, but I'm starving."

He headed for the kitchen area and extracted an ironstone baking dish from the oven. "Lasagna!" he announced proudly. "I made it myself."

"I'm impressed." Holly pulled out a chair at the table and paused to admire the swooping grace of sculptured wood.

"I made that chair myself, too," Philip said. "And the table. I made most of the furniture in this place." He took a huge glass bowl of salad from the refrigerator and placed it on the round wooden table.

Holly slid her hand across the glossy surface of it. "Beautiful," she said.

"Walnut," he replied. "Works fairly easily and takes a good polish. I used to be a carpenter by trade. Fine woodworking was my specialty."

"A carpenter?" Holly found this bit of information comforting. At least he hadn't been born rich. But she'd already guessed that. For all his apparent wealth, Philip still had rough edges. Unlike his glossy furniture, he'd kept his own surface natural and unpolished. And that appealed to Holly. "So how'd you make it from modest carpenter to Condominium King?" she asked.

"Well, that's a long story."

"Another long story? You answered the same way when I asked why you cared so much about the goddess."

The moment Holly said that, she wished she hadn't. She didn't want to talk about the goddess now. For the first time since she'd purchased the figure, she wasn't carrying it with her. She told herself she hadn't brought it for the simple reason that her dress had no pockets. But it wasn't that simple. Bringing the goddess along would have been like bringing a rival to share Philip's attention. That was silly, she knew, yet the thought *had* crossed her mind.

"Most personal stories are long if you tell the whole truth and don't leave anything out," Philip told her. "I don't want to bore you."

"I doubt you could ever bore me, Philip, even if you tried," Holly replied.

He smiled. "You have a way of saying the nicest, most unexpected things, Mrs. Murphey."

Holly lifted her shoulders. "I only tell the truth."

"You don't play games, do you?"

She smiled at him a bit wistfully. "I never even learned the rules."

"The games I'm talking about don't have any rules."

And he's probably a master at them, Holly thought. She broke his gaze and stared at the table. It was set with thick blue plates on rush mats, heavy silverware and wineglasses and white linen napkins. A pickle jar containing three red tulips sat in the center. Holly reached out and touched a glossy petal.

"Those are the only three that have come up in the garden so far this spring," Philip told her. "I couldn't resist picking them for you."

It had been a long time since a man had picked flowers for her. Or made dinner for her. She glanced at Philip suspiciously as he opened a bottle of Chianti. Was he giving her this special treatment because he wanted her Goddess of Joy? Or did he really like her? His two brief kisses had seemed so spontaneous and natural. Or were they part of his game plan? If he tried kissing her again, she would voice a firm objection, she decided.

"Let's have a sample of this lasagna of yours," she said in a challenging tone. "I should warn you that my grandmother was Italian."

"Hey! So was one of mine." Philip took her plate and gave her a huge serving. "On my mother's side. My father's mother was Polish. My grandfathers were French and English. I come from a mixed bag of nationalities. I'm a mongrel like King."

He stated it so proudly that Holly had to smile. "Well, so am I," she declared. "Russian, Irish, Italian and English."

He served himself and joined her at the table. After pouring each of them a generous glass of wine, he raised his. "Here's to America's melting pot."

Holly drank to that.

"You're certainly a beautiful product of it," Philip added, ignoring his wine and drinking in her face instead. "High Slavic cheekbones, poetic Irish eyes, sensual Botticelli lips and—"

"Stop!" Holly interrupted. "You're embarrassing me, Philip."

"And prim English reserve," he concluded. "I intend to break through that reserve of yours one of these days, cautious Mrs. Murphey." He gave her a disarming grin. "Pass the salad, please."

They ate in silence for a while as Holly digested Philip's stated intention. He impressed her as a man who usually accomplished what he proposed. He couldn't know, though, how deeply she had buried herself in layers of protection. Her heart felt as encased as...a tulip bud. She glanced at the three blooming tulips that Philip had picked for her. Plants could come to life after a long period of dormancy. But could people?

"Why so quiet, Holly? Is the lasagna *that* bad?"

She made an effort to smile. "It's delicious. Even better than my grandmother's. And that's the highest praise I can give it."

"I like to cook," he said, pleased. "I like creating something out of raw materials. That's why I enjoy working with wood, too. I was never happier than when I made a living with my hands."

Holly's eyes drifted down to his large, big-knuckled hands. They looked strong and competent, yet oddly graceful, too, with long, tapered fingers. "Then why did you give up the carpentry trade?"

"Money," Philip replied succinctly. He took a sip of wine and sighed. "Tell me, Holly. What was your dream when you were twenty or so?"

To marry the love of her life and live happily ever after. Such a simple answer, but one she could not bear to utter. She tossed her head and attempted a casual smile. "I can't remember that far back."

"Oh, come on. You're not that old."

"I'm thirty-three," she told him. "No spring chicken."

Philip laughed. "Hell, I'm five years older! So what does that make me—a decrepit rooster?"

"Hardly. You're obviously a man in the prime of life, Mr. Irons." Although her tone was teasing, she meant every word.

"There you go again. Saying something nice."

"And you were fishing again."

He nodded and laughed. "Well, you didn't have to swallow the bait."

Holly took a sip of wine. It warmed her. And despite her misgivings, she couldn't help warming up to Philip. She found his company much more relaxing than she'd expected. At the moment, at least, she felt completely comfortable with him. "Okay, have it your way," she said. "You're a decrepit rooster."

He grimaced, then smiled ruefully. "It's funny how the years creep up on you. I always assumed that I'd have a family by this time in my life. Instead, here I am, living all alone in my tower."

"Poor Philip," Holly said lightly, but she didn't like the way the conversation was going.

"Oh, I'm not asking for sympathy," he said. "Life's been good to me. But I really like kids, you know. Maybe because I come from such a large family. What about you, Holly?"

"No, I don't come from a large family. Only one brother," she replied, deflecting the point of his question. "I'd like to hear more about your work, Philip."

He studied her a long moment, as if considering whether to pursue the topic of family. Apparently he decided not to. "I've been trying to get a pet project of mine off the ground for months, but I'm having trouble financing it," he said.

Holly looked surprised. "Why? Your company is a proven success, isn't it?"

"That's part of the problem. Investors want me to continue doing the same thing, but I'm tired of building luxury condominium developments. I'd like to concentrate on building less expensive ones. Housing prices have become outrageous in this area, especially for couples just starting out."

Holly could see it so vividly at that moment—the modest ranch house she and Daniel had bought right after Danny was born. Their palace! Because they could barely afford the mortgage payments on Daniel's income, she'd planned to go back to work to ease their tight budget once Daniel entered first grade. He'd never made it to first grade.

Philip went on about the rising cost of real estate but stopped when he noticed Holly's faraway expression. "I guess you underestimated my ability to bore you, Holly."

Holly yanked herself back to the present. "You aren't!" Surely she was the boring one, she thought. She hadn't meant to slip into the past like that, for even a moment. She wished Philip hadn't noticed her slight lapse. "Please tell me more about this project of yours."

He shook his head. "Maybe later. But right now I have a confession to make."

Holly wasn't sure she wanted to hear it. It would only tempt her to divulge personal information to him, too, and she didn't know him well enough for that. Perhaps she never would.

Her fears were quickly extinguished when Philip proceeded with his disclosure. "I didn't make dessert. But I've got some vanilla ice cream in the freezer. How about a dish of that? And coffee."

"Vanilla is my favorite," she told him, relieved to keep things light. "And I like my coffee black."

"Ah, a purist like me." Philip gave her an approving smile.

And Holly melted a little inside under the beam of it. She was finding it more and more difficult to deny the attraction she felt for this man. She'd felt it the moment he'd stalked into her classroom, and she'd immediately become defensive. She wasn't ready for it. A year from now, maybe even six months from now, she might be. But not now! The immediacy of Philip's attraction frightened her a little.

While he was occupied making coffee, Holly wandered into the sitting area and made herself comfortable on the sofa beside the snoring King Kong. He shifted his position to snuggle against her, and Holly automatically began stroking his head. She had a warm spot in her heart for homely mutts. Danny had brought one home under his winter jacket when he was five. He'd found it abandoned in a vacant lot next door to their house. Against her better judgment she'd agreed to let the dog spend the night. What else could a mother say to a little boy with big, pleading eyes who was clutching a shivering puppy to his heart?

Daniel had come home late that evening from a sales trip that hadn't been as successful as he'd hoped. He'd shaken his head over the pitiful sight of the pup, huddled on a blanket in the kitchen, and told Holly that a sickly mutt was the last thing they needed. She'd fully agreed. They would have to tell Danny the next morning that the dog couldn't stay. But then Daniel had gone into Danny's bedroom, touched his sleeping face and turned to Holly with the same pleading look that their son had given her. It had cost them hundreds of dollars in vet bills, but the dog had survived. Danny had named him Lucky.

"Careful, it's hot," Philip said, leaning over Holly to offer her a steaming mug of coffee.

Startled out of her reverie, she shifted so quickly that she knocked the mug out of his hand with her shoulder. It landed on the rug without breaking, but the coffee splattered everywhere. Holly jumped to her feet and ran to the kitchen area for a towel. She returned and dropped to her knees to mop up the spill.

"How clumsy of me," she muttered.

Philip knelt beside her and tried to take the towel from her. "Let me do that, Holly."

"No, no, let me."

Each determined to clean up the mess, they had a tugging match with the towel. King, barking with great enthusiasm, leaped from the sofa and onto Holly, knocking her backward. She fell against Philip's chest, pushing him down, too, and King, now delighted beyond reason with the game, tussled with both of them on the rug.

"Don't be afraid. He's just playing," Philip said.

Holly turned her face aside to avoid another swipe from King's wagging tail, but she wasn't afraid. She was laughing. It had been a long time since she'd been part of such spontaneous horseplay—or dog play. Tumbling fracases on the floor with Lucky and Daniel and Danny had once been part of the Murphey family's nightly entertainment.

Philip put a stop to this one by throwing the towel across the room. King bounded for it, paws skidding along the floorboards. He shook his limp prey in his mighty jaws, then lay down with a contented sigh and gnawed at it.

"Sorry about that, Holly," Philip said, sitting up. "King Kong goes crazy at the sight of a dish towel. It's like waving a red flag in front of..." His words drifted away as he gazed at Holly, still on her back and laughing, her skirt tangled around her thighs. "Lord, you are so beautiful," he whispered.

The laughter caught in her throat as he leaned over her, closer and closer, his gray eyes glittering with intensity. Before she could catch her breath, much less her good sense, their lips met.

The gentle persuasiveness of his kiss disarmed Holly completely. She closed her eyes, and her mouth softened against his. She'd forgotten the thrill of a first kiss, and the innate sweetness of this initial, tentative exploration. Philip tasted so good to her, smelled so good. She wrapped her arms around his neck, pulling him closer. The male weight against her breasts was so familiar, yet so strange. No man had held her like this since Daniel. Her body seemed to thaw against the warmth of Philip's chest.

"So beautiful," he whispered again, and his breath tingled in her ear, tingled through her. He smoothed her hair and kissed her temple, her cheekbone, the long sweep of her neck.

Holly arched her back a little to press closer to him, and that subtle gesture of compliance encouraged him to capture her lips again with more urgency and intensity. Their kiss deepened, and Holly felt the heat of desire flow through her. It had been so long, so long.

Too long! Her sudden passion, so easily stoked by this man, this *stranger*, embarrassed her. She averted her flushed face and pushed her palms against Philip's shoulders. "Don't," she commanded in a barely audible voice.

He pulled away from her immediately, and she felt suddenly cold without the pressure of his warm, solid body against hers. He looked at her with a frown of...puzzlement? anger? disappointment? If she didn't even know him well enough to interpret his expression, how could she have wanted him so much, so quickly? How could she have lost herself to him like that for even a moment? She hadn't meant to lead him on in any way.

"I'm sorry," she said.

"For what?" With brisk agility, Philip stood and offered her his hand. She took it, and he pulled her to her feet. He smiled tightly and smoothed down his tie. "A kiss is nothing to be sorry about, Holly. It was a highly enjoyable experience. Now how about that ice cream?" He turned and headed to the kitchen.

Holly was relieved that he'd left it at that—a simple pleasure shared then dismissed without the slightest need for explanations. At the same time a smoky curl of disappointment wafted through her. Was kissing her that easily dismissed?

She returned to the sofa, and Philip joined her shortly, bringing more coffee and dessert. Holly liked watching him eat his ice cream. He seemed to take such simple pleasure in it. He exuded a certain youthful vitality that Holly found extremely appealing. His eyebrows slanted slightly, giving him an expectant, quizzical expression, and joined with the narrow bridge of his nose. But his eyes were far too sharp and clever and penetrating to be considered boyish. More silver than gray, really, she observed. Quicksilver eyes. Unpredictable.

He licked his spoon, and the flash of his tongue unsettled her. How delicious it would taste now, cold and sweet from the ice cream. Holly, stop! she enjoined herself. She couldn't stop thinking about it, though. She couldn't stop recalling the thrilling sensation of his kisses, first gentle and soothing, then excitingly greedy. But his demeanor was so casual now that she could almost doubt that it had really happened.

She forced her eyes away from him and concentrated on eating her own melting ice cream. She was glad that it slid down her throat so easily, because she had lost her appetite for food. Philip's kiss had made her acutely aware that she craved another sort of nourishment. The knowledge shocked her. She'd assumed her passion had been buried with Daniel. She'd never considered that she could respond to another man. Yet she had. And she knew that if Philip kissed her again, she would respond even more strongly.

"I'm not going to keep you waiting any longer, Holly," Philip announced, and his spoon made a loud ringing sound as he tossed it in the bowl.

She laughed awkwardly. Surely he wasn't capable of reading her thoughts. "Waiting for what?"

"Aren't you impatient to see my netsuke collection?"

She'd all but forgotten that was her reason for coming to his home. She rose, put on an expectant look and glanced at the spiral staircase that led to his bedroom. "Up there, right?"

Philip nodded, smiling. "You go up first. The stairs are tricky, but you'll get used to them."

Did he mean after a few steps or a few climbs? she wondered. She held onto the cold iron banister as she mounted the stairs but made the mistake of looking down through the open spaces between them. Caught a little off balance, she swayed. Philip, close behind, placed his hands on her waist to steady her. She felt instantly safe and secure.

The room at the top of the stairs was as large and simply furnished as the one below. A king-size bed, mounted on a pale wood platform and covered with a bright red comforter, dominated it.

"The view up here is terrific," Philip said, moving toward one of the long arched windows and beckoning her.

Holly joined him. The stars were bright in the clear night sky and seemed to be reflected below by the dots of light emanating from the condominium units.

"You can see for miles in the daytime," Philip told her. "The first thing I do when I wake up is look out this window. Seeing the world from above puts it all back into perspective for me. All my problems and worries dwindle in importance. I like being up high. Ever been in a hot-air balloon, Holly?"

She shook her head. "I have a fear of heights," she admitted.

"Who doesn't? But you'll get over it once you're aloft. You'll love it, I promise you."

Was he promising to take her for a ride in a hot-air balloon? Holly wondered. Or only assuring her that if she ever found herself in one, which seemed highly unlikely, she would enjoy it?

Without another word he took her hand and led her toward his bed. Then past it, to a tall display cabinet. It was a graceful structure of mahogany fronted by glass. The felt-lined shelves were crowded with tiny carved figures. Philip opened the glass door and took one out.

"From the eighteenth century," he told Holly, handing it to her.

She turned the jade figure in her hands, both fascinated and repulsed. It was part dragon, part snake, with the head of a man, mouth opened wide. She laughed uncomfortably. "What a monster!"

"Shokuin," Philip said. "He rules day and night and the changing seasons. It's quite a lovely piece once you get used to it."

Holly handed it back to him. "Interesting," she managed to say.

Philip grinned. "But too fierce for your taste, right? Here's a more pleasant god." He gave her an ivory figure of a fat-bellied, bald, laughing man with two children climbing around his bulk. "Hotei," Philip said. "He symbolizes prosperity, contentment and good nature."

This netsuke charmed Holly. As did a sleeping cat on a leaf-shaped fan, a dancing fox, a cheerful woman carrying wash on her head, even a fantastic being with the body of a turtle, frog's legs and a monkey's head.

"A *baku*," Philip informed her. "They're mischievous creatures that carry their power in bowls on top of their heads, and they can cause a lot of trouble if they come into your life. But I'll give you a tip on how to get rid of one."

"Please do," Holly said. "The last thing I need in my life is a pesky *baku*."

"You do this." Philip bowed to her.

"That's it? You bow?"

"*Baku* are extremely polite and will always bow back. The liquid runs out of the bowl, and they lose their power. It's as simple as that."

"Thanks for the tip," Holly said. Her laughing eyes glowed as she looked at Philip. "Who knows? There could be a *baku* waiting for me around the very next corner."

"Anything's possible. It's always best to be prepared."

"Yes, anything can happen at any time," she agreed softly as the merriment drained from her eyes. "Things can happen that you're totally unprepared for."

Her sudden seriousness caused Philip to frown. "Like what, Holly?"

She shrugged. "Anything."

"But you were referring to something specific and personal. Your husband's death?"

"I'd rather not talk about it, if you don't mind."

"Of course not." Philip ran his hand through her hair. "You'll tell me about it when you're ready." He cupped her pale cheek in his palm for a brief moment, then turned his attention to the case. "Here's the Hojitsu netsuke I told you about, Holly. The prize of my collection." He laid it in her palm. "Isn't she exquisite? The Ama. The diving fisherwoman of Japan."

Holly appreciated the supreme beauty of the piece. The figure of a graceful woman seemed to flow out of the intricate oyster shell carved around her feet. "Exquisite," she agreed.

"You can have my Ama and the money I already offered you if you give me the Goddess of Joy."

Holly's heart sank with the belief that he'd been setting her up all evening for this moment. "No," she said.

"Then choose another piece, Holly. Any one in this case. They're all museum quality, I assure you."

"I don't want to trade or sell my goddess."

Philip gave her a long, hard stare. "Very well," he finally said. He offered his hand to her, palm up, and for an instant Holly thought he wanted her to place hers in it as a gesture of friendship. But then she understood that he only wanted the Ama back. Ignoring his hand, she replaced the netsuke in the case herself.

"I think it's time I was going," she said.

"Please don't rush off." His voice expressed only the utmost politeness. "We can have more coffee. Or brandy if you'd like."

He sounded so stiff and formal. "No, I've stayed long enough," she replied as stiffly. "Thank you for showing me your collection, Philip. I learned a lot. And thank you for dinner, too. It was very good."

"You're welcome," he replied. "I'd like to have dinner with you again soon."

"Sure you would." She attempted a laugh. It came out harsh and false. "How many dinners do you think it'll take to get my netsuke from me?" How many kisses? she silently added. She felt like a fool for responding so strongly.

He narrowed his eyes. "You can't still believe that's the only reason I asked you here tonight?"

"Oh, I'm not complaining." She put on a brave smile and hoped he didn't notice how it trembled at the edges. "I got a tour, a free dinner and a netsuke lecture. But I don't think we should get together again. Goodbye, Philip."

She turned from him abruptly and headed for the stairway, accidentally brushing against the side of his big bed as she passed it.

"Holly, wait. You're not being fair to me."

She didn't wait. Her heels made a clattering sound as she hurried down the iron steps, gripping the banister tightly. She wasn't sure if she could find her way to the front door. He'd led her through such a labyrinth to get to the tower. But she needn't have worried about that. He followed her down and insisted on walking her to her car.

At least it hadn't turned into a pumpkin, she mused when they went outside. They hadn't exchanged a word since leaving Philip's bedroom. "Well, goodbye again," she said and had the grace to offer him her hand this time.

He took it immediately. "Stop fooling yourself, Holly, because you're not fooling me," he told her softly. "You're not upset because I asked you to sell the netsuke again. You're just using that as an excuse to be angry with me and nip what we started in the bud. It's not the goddess you're afraid of losing." He leaned closer, so close that she could feel his breath on her face. "It's your heart."

"Ridiculous!" She attempted to yank her hand from his, but he kept a firm hold. "I didn't realize how conceited you were, Philip."

"Just direct and honest." He pulled her hand to his lips and kissed the inside of her wrist, where her pulse beat fast and furious. Then he released her hand as if it were a bird he was setting free. "Good night, Mrs. Murphey. Drive carefully. You'll be hearing from me soon."

She ran down the front steps and got into her car without looking back. But she couldn't resist a glance in her rearview mirror as she headed down the drive. The sight of his broad-shouldered frame, silhouetted against the light of the open doorway as he watched her depart, sent a thrill through her. She tore her eyes from the mirror and concentrated on the road ahead.

Chapter Five

The Murpheys always ate Sunday dinner at noon. The menu never varied. Grace Murphey always overcooked the pot roast and undercooked the potatoes and carrots. Her gravy never failed to be lumpy; her lemon meringue pie was usually too runny. Still, all week Holly looked forward to Sunday dinner at the Murphey home. It was her link to her past, to all her past happiness.

Her parents-in-law, Grace and Mike, lived in Milford, a suburb of New Haven. Holly had grown up on the same street, two doors down from the Murpheys. The three Murphey daughters were older than she, and she'd always been closest to Daniel, their youngest child and only son.

When Holly arrived at the house at eleven, Mike waved to her from the driveway. He was washing his car.

"Hey, gorgeous! Gorgeous day, huh?" he called as she pulled in.

Holly got out and gave him a warm hug. He had a round, jovial face, a bald head and a big stomach. Daniel used to teasingly refer to his father's stomach as his pot-roast pot. It struck Holly now how much Mike resembled the netsuke of Hotei that Philip had shown her the night before. She blinked away that fancy. She didn't want to think about Philip, even indirectly. Not now. Not while she was with the Murpheys.

"What's for dinner today?" she asked Mike.

It was the family's traditional Sunday joke, and he let out a laugh. "Would you believe lobster?"

"No," Holly said. "Who's coming?"

"Just Celia and you. Seems everybody else had better things to do today. It's not like it used to be now that most of the grandchildren are teenagers." Mike looked glum as he dipped a sponge in a bucket of soapy water but was smiling again as he squeezed it out. "Not that I got anything to complain about now that you're here, honey. I can feast my eyes on your pretty face during the meal."

"Oh, Mike. Have you been kissing the blarney stone again?"

"I'd rather kiss you." He gave her a smack on the cheek. His twinkling eyes became serious in the next instant. "You know, Holly, you shouldn't feel obliged to come here every Sunday if *you* have better things to do."

"But I don't, Mike. There's no place I'd rather be than here."

"Well, good. Great!" He slapped her back for emphasis. "We love ya like a daughter, honey." He went back to washing his car, whistling tunelessly but with great enthusiasm. Mike wasn't one to waste time conversing when there was a job to be done.

Holly entered the house through the kitchen door. She could smell the roast cooking and imagined it shriveling in the covered pan. Grace, small and slender, peeled potatoes at the sink while her eldest daughter, Celia, sat at the table painting her nails orchid. Celia was a tall, heavy-set, handsome woman with exceptionally dainty hands and feet. She had an abrupt, know-it-all demeanor that sometimes put Holly off.

"As usual, Ma's late getting the potatoes on, Hol," Celia announced in lieu of a greeting. "They'll be hard as stones."

Ignoring her daughter's criticism, Grace wiped her hands on her terry-cloth apron and grabbed both of Holly's, squeezing them tightly. "Hello, honey. How are you?"

"Just fine." Holly bent to kiss Grace's cheek. "What can I do to help?"

"Not a thing. Everything's under control."

"My divorce became final yesterday," Celia told Holly as she carefully coated another fingernail.

"That's nothing to brag about, Ce," her mother said.

"I'm not bragging, Ma. I'm stating a fact. Besides, divorce is nothing to be ashamed of. Right, Hol?"

Holly certainly didn't think it was but she also appreciated Grace's feelings. Rather than take sides, she didn't answer but asked Celia how her two boys were doing instead.

"They're hanging out with their father today," Celia replied. "They seem to prefer Sam's company to mine lately and keep threatening to move in with him. Sure. Why not?" Her voice rose. "He lets them get away with bloody murder!"

"Take it easy, hon," Grace cautioned. "It's healthy for boys to spend time with their father. The ideal, of course, would be to have both parents living together."

"Yeah, but guess what, Ma. Life isn't as perfect as you'd like it to be." With that Celia stalked off to the living room, taking her bottle of nail polish with her.

"Oh, dear," Grace said, wringing her apron. "It seems I always say the wrong thing to Celia lately. Why don't you go keep her company, Holly? Maybe you can put her in a better mood."

Holly doubted it. Celia was seven years older, and they'd never been close friends. But she couldn't refuse Grace's request and dutifully went into the living room. Celia had slipped off her sandals and was now painting her toenails. She glanced up when Holly entered.

"Hol, turn on the radio, will you?" It was more a command than a request.

Holly complied. Celia used to baby-sit for her when she was a kid, and Holly was accustomed to her bossiness. The radio sat on a bulky credenza crowded with framed family photographs, and Holly paused to examine them. She'd gazed at them hundreds of times before, but they never failed to capture her interest. She smiled at the formal wedding portrait of Daniel and herself, remembering how he'd kept patting her behind and making her giggle as they'd posed for it. Then she picked up her favorite photograph of Daniel and Danny in a rowboat. Danny, grinning proudly, was holding up the trout he'd caught. Like his father, he'd been an avid fisherman. If only they hadn't been so crazy about the sport. If only...

"Holly," Celia said in a softer, more kindly tone than usual. "Put that picture down and come talk to me." She patted the faded sofa cushion beside her. "I want to tell you all about my new boyfriend."

"Your boyfriend?"

Celia made a wry face. "I know it sounds corny for a forty-year-old woman to have a boyfriend, but I really don't know what else to call him. I mean, he isn't my lover. Yet." She glanced toward the kitchen and lowered her voice. "We're still at the hand-holding stage, but I may have an affair with him. Heck, why not? I'm free as a bird now that my divorce is final."

Holly settled down on the sofa. "You don't want to rush into anything, Ce," she cautioned.

"Of course *you'd* say that." Celia sighed. "You haven't even thought about seeing another man since you lost Daniel, have you?"

Holly hesitated. "It's recently crossed my mind."

Celia leaned closer, interested. "Have you met someone special?"

Holly looked away. She didn't want to discuss Philip with Daniel's sister, of all people.

"So there is someone special," Celia said, either reading Holly's expression or interpreting her silence as an admission. She waved away Holly's impending protest. "I'm glad for you, Hol. I truly am. You know how much I adored my little brother. But your life has to go on without him."

"My life *has* gone on," Holly insisted. She absently put her hand in the pocket of her slacks and palmed the Goddess of Joy. "I have a job I enjoy, which gives me great satisfaction. Under the circumstances, I think I've adjusted quite well."

"I didn't mean to imply that you haven't, Hol. Heck, everybody in the family always comments on how brave and stoic and well adjusted you are. Nobody mentions that you've lived like a nun for the past four years, though."

"Really, Celia. You have no way of knowing that."

"Oh, stop blushing, Holly. I've known you since you were in diapers, and I can read you like a book. I even know the exact moment you fell in love with Daniel."

Holly laughed at that. She didn't know herself.

"It was at the lake," Celia continued. "You were eleven or so, still flat as a board but parading around in a two-piece bathing suit like you were Miss America, using the wharf as your ramp." She chuckled. "You used to be such a hot ticket, Hol. We never knew what crazy stunt you'd be pulling next. Anyway, Daniel followed you up the wharf and slipped a minnow down your top. You shoved him into the lake and ran to the cottage sobbing. That's when I knew you two loved each other, and I bet you knew it, too."

"I don't even remember that," Holly said, amazed that she didn't.

"Oh." Celia's face dropped. "Well, that was the summer your parents got divorced, and maybe that's what you remember most about it. You took it pretty hard."

"I sure did," Holly admitted. "I was so angry with them that I wanted to disown them and have your parents adopt me. It took me a while to understand that they made the right decision."

"I hope my boys will understand some day." Celia put a freshly painted fingernail to her mouth and scraped it with her teeth. "Sometimes I wonder if I shouldn't have stuck out my marriage to the bitter end. Or at least until the boys left home."

"Oh, Celia, children sense the bitterness, believe me. I'm certainly glad my parents didn't stick it out for my sake. Then nobody would have been happy. Give your boys time. They'll come around. Take it from somebody who knows."

Celia smiled wanly. "Funny, but I never thought I'd be listening to advice from the bratty kid I used to baby-sit. Remember the time you and Daniel stole my diary?"

"Now that I do remember, Ce! Quite vividly." Holly found great delight in taking these trips down memory lane with the Murpheys. "You had to chase us around the block three times before you caught us."

"Oh, you were such a little devil. I used to tell Ma that you were a bad influence on my precious baby brother."

"Daniel was no angel himself, Ce. Half the pranks we pulled were his idea, not mine."

"Yeah, you used to call yourselves the Double Dares. Ma always said that the two of you had a match made in heaven and—" She bit her bottom lip to stop herself. "Sorry, Hol. I didn't mean to get maudlin."

"Don't apologize. I love talking about Daniel."

Celia nodded. "Is that the reason you come here every Sunday? I'm sure it's not Ma's cooking that keeps bringing you back."

"I come because I'm fond of your parents. I'm fond of all the Murpheys." She smiled. "Even you, Ce."

Celia smiled back. "Maybe we should get together for lunch sometime."

"I'd like that."

"Heck, maybe we could even double-date."

Holly waved off the last suggestion. "Let's not get carried away."

"No, seriously. My boyfriend—his name is Frank, by the way—loves to go bowling. And I remember how much you loved it, too, in the old days. Does this guy you're interested in know how to bowl?"

"I never said I was interested in anyone, Celia. You're as bad as my students about jumping to conclusions."

"So they've noticed the change in you, too. I certainly have. And even Ma and Pa remarked about how much happier you've been looking these past few weeks."

"They're right. I've been happier lately," Holly allowed. "But it has nothing to do with Philip. I just met him a few days ago."

Celia pointed her index finger at Holly. "Gotcha!"

Holly couldn't help but laugh. Philip's name had a way of slipping off her tongue. She'd spent a sleepless night thinking about him, replaying their evening together over and over again in her mind, glossing over their kiss and then going back and dwelling on it. Safe in her bed, she'd regretted leaving his home so hastily. Perhaps she'd overreacted when he'd offered to buy the goddess again. She'd surely overreacted to his kiss. She would have to keep a tighter rein on her emotions the next time she saw him, she'd concluded by dawn. Then she'd rolled over and fallen fast asleep, having no doubt that she would be seeing him again. If there was one thing she knew for certain about Philip Irons, it was that he never gave up.

"So tell me more about this Philip," Celia demanded.

"Oh, I'd rather hear about Frank," Holly said.

And for the next half hour or so that's all Holly did hear about. She listened attentively as Celia gushed, and felt pleased that she had managed to put Celia in a better mood, after all. When the telephone rang Celia stopped in midsentence and leaped up to answer it. Her mood improved even more when she found out who was calling.

"How'd you know I'd be here, Frank?" she asked with surprised delight. "Oh, right. I told you."

As Celia giggled over what Frank said next, Holly quietly left the room and joined Grace in the kitchen.

"Is Celia still glum?" Grace asked.

"No, she's perked up considerably."

Holly took the platter of pot roast and vegetables into the dining room. When she returned to the kitchen Celia and Grace were having a spat.

"What's the big deal?" Celia was saying. "So I skip Sunday dinner with you? The world won't stop turning."

"Well, I just don't understand why you have to rush off like this. Who were you talking to on the phone? That Frank person you've been seeing?"

"Ma, he's got a last name. And he's a real gentleman. He asked me to go watch him and his team play softball in the park." She smiled. "I think he wants to show off in front of me. It's nice to have a man pay attention to me again. Is that so terrible, Ma?"

"No," Grace allowed after a moment. "You go and have a good time, Celia. Make sure you say goodbye to Pa and thank him for washing your car."

"I begged him not to. It wasn't even dirty."

"It makes him feel useful," Grace said.

"Maybe he can start a car wash when he retires." Celia gave her mother a quick kiss and waved to Holly. "Let's go on that double date soon, Hol," she said before rushing out the back door.

Grace took the rolls out of the oven. As always, they were burned on the bottom. She looked at Holly. "Double date?" she asked casually.

"I wish Celia hadn't said that in front of you."

"Why not, honey? You don't think Mike or I would mind if you started dating, do you? My goodness,

Holly, we don't expect you to spend the rest of your life in mourning."

"I never think in terms of the *rest* of my life. I don't like to think about the future at all, Grace."

"That's fine. Live in the present." Grace brushed her hand against Holly's arm. "But don't dwell on the past, honey."

Holly nodded and swallowed hard. "I haven't had those horrible nightmares about Danny for months." She could only speak about her son here in the Murphey house.

"That's good," Grace said in a thick voice. She cleared her throat. "Put those rolls in the basket, will you, honey? And then run out and tell Mike that dinner's on the table."

"Good lemon pie, Grace," her husband declared after polishing off his slice of it.

"A bit runny," she commented, as she usually did, with good reason.

"I wouldn't have it any other way. That's the pie I'm used to, and that's the pie I like!" Mike stated forcefully.

Holly found great comfort in the predictability of the conversation. It seemed strange to be having dinner alone with them, though. For as long as Holly could remember, there had never been fewer than five family members at the table, sometimes as many as twenty knocking shoulders and elbows in the dining room and kitchen.

Mike threw down his napkin and rose, adjusting his belt around his bulk. "Well, I got things to do, ladies. You two have a nice gab session." He left the dining room and went out the kitchen door. Through the window Holly could see him pacing the small backyard.

Grace watched him, too, and shook her head. "He's at loose ends today. He misses the grandchildren." She touched her grandmother brooch, which she always wore on Sunday. It had ten tiny gems in it—the birthstones of her ten grandchildren. Holly's eyes always went directly to the sapphire, which represented Danny.

"Well, everyone will probably show up next Sunday," she said.

Grace sniffed. "It would be nice if one of my daughters offered to have dinner at her house for a change."

Her remark took Holly by surprise. It had never occurred to her that Grace would appreciate a change in the routine.

"Not that I'm complaining," Grace quickly amended. "I'm thankful we're such a tight-knit family. But honestly, Holly, there are some Sundays when I don't want to face another pot roast. I recently suggested to Mike that we drive to a country inn for dinner after church, just the two of us, and he looked so shocked you'd think I'd suggested something blasphemous." She laughed. "Sort of the way you're looking at me now, honey."

Holly tried to adjust her expression. "But having dinner here is such a family tradition, Grace."

"Oh, pooh." She stood and began clearing the table. "Sometimes I think tradition is just an excuse for staying in a rut." With that she marched to the kitchen.

Holly picked up the remaining plates and followed her. She didn't know what to say. Grace didn't sound like herself at all.

"How do your mother and stepfather like Florida?" Grace asked her, seemingly out of the blue, as she tied her apron around her waist.

"They're very happy there. They play golf every day."

"Hmm." Grace filled the sink with water and looked out the window dreamily. "I wonder if Mike would enjoy golf. We could learn the game together. He's going to retire next month, you know. I'll certainly have my hands full then!" She plunged them in the dishwater.

"You're not thinking of moving to Florida, are you?" Holly asked apprehensively.

"Oh, I don't know." Grace rinsed a dish and handed it to Holly to dry. "I've been looking into it. Arizona and California, too. A change of scenery would do Mike a world of good." Her eyes lifted to the window above the sink again. "Look at him out there, Holly. He's washing *your* car now. He needs some new interests in life."

"But he'd missed the grandchildren so much."

"Oh, honey, he's going to miss them whether we move or not. They're all getting too old to follow Grandpa around on Sunday. Why, even Danny, the youngest, would have been..." Grace's voice caught.

"Ten," Holly said softly. "He would have been ten now. Eleven in September."

"Ah, yes. My precious sapphire." Grace touched the tiny birthstone on her brooch with a damp fingertip. "His eyes were as deep a blue."

They finished the dishes in silence. Then Grace told Holly she had a surprise for her and led her to the front porch, where there was a large brown box taped closed.

"What's this?" Holly asked. On closer examination she noticed her own mother's handwriting on the top of it. Holly's High School Mementos. "How in the world did you end up with this, Grace?"

"As I recall, your mom dropped it off right before moving to Florida. You and Daniel were on your honeymoon, so Mike took it up to the attic, where it's been sitting all these years. Mike was rummaging up there yesterday and discovered it. We thought you'd want to have it."

Holly wasn't sure she did. Powerful memories of Daniel were contained in that box. They'd gone steady all through high school. But she couldn't very well ask Grace to keep storing it in her attic. Or tell her to throw it out. "Thanks." She picked it up. "I'll put it in the trunk of my car right now."

"Mike will carry it out for you when you're ready to leave."

"I can manage. It's bulky but light," Holly said with a heavy heart.

When Holly returned to New Haven later that afternoon, the only parking space she could find was three blocks from her apartment, and she decided to leave the box in her trunk for the time being. She had little inclination to delve into it. Her visit to the Murpheys every Sunday satisfied her need to relive memories of her past happiness, and she tried not to dwell on them during the rest of the week. With the passage of time it had become less and less of an effort.

Back at her apartment, she made herself a pot of coffee, and while it was brewing she sprinkled food into a glass bowl for her two goldfish. She missed having a dog around and sometimes regretted that she'd given Lucky to her brother in Vermont. But the poor dog had been so miserable without Danny, and it had pained Holly to watch him wait by the door all day, week after week, for the little boy's return. Now Lucky had other children to play with—Holly's nieces.

Holly's apartment had nothing in it to remind her of Daniel and Danny. She'd sold the ranch house five months after the funeral and donated all the furniture to the Salvation Army, along with her husband's and son's clothing and Danny's new bicycle and toys. She'd even donated the pots and pans she'd used to cook meals for them, the dishes they'd used, the pastel double-bed sheets and the sheets for the single bed imprinted with cartoon characters. No one could stop her from doing this, although Grace and her own mother had tried to reason with her. But she'd been unreasonable, driven by pain and an anger so great that sometimes she thought she would explode. She'd been unable to get rid of this anger for a long time because she had nothing to direct it against except fate.

Now Holly roamed her sparsely furnished apartment, watering her plants as the coffee perked. She kept thinking about the box in the trunk of her car. She would eventually have to retrieve it, she knew. She decided to put it deep in her bedroom closet, where it would join another unopened box containing a wedding album, baby pictures, a stuffed Mickey Mouse, a child's scuffed baseball mitt, a man's faded flannel shirt and a wedding band. That was all she had left of her husband and child. That and her weekly visits to the Murpheys.

They might move away! This thought froze Holly in the motion of watering a hanging maidenhair fern. Had Grace been serious about that? she wondered. Surely Mike wouldn't go along with such a plan. Yet perhaps Grace was right—a change would do him good. Mike and Grace had devoted their lives to their family, and maybe it was time for them to let go and start afresh. Holly felt a slap of water against her cheek. It had overflowed from the planter saucer. She immediately tilted up the spout of her plastic watering can and hurried to the kitchen for paper towels, frowning with irritation.

A smile suddenly replaced Holly's frown as she remembered another recent spill and King Kong going crazy over the sight of a dish towel. Her smile softened as she remembered Philip leaning over her...lowering his face to hers...kissing her. She stood in the kitchen, clutching a paper towel, oblivious to the drip, drip, drip of the overflowing planter.

Philip stood in the vast foyer of his showy mansion, bidding good-night to his dinner guests Sunday evening. He couldn't wait for them to leave. He found formal dinners tedious, and he'd been the host of far too many of them lately. This one had dragged on longer than he'd expected, but his smile remained amiable as he chatted with his departing guests. Giles Grant and his daughter Vivian were the last to leave.

"Oh, dear!" Vivian said. "I left my purse in the dining room. Be an angel and get it for me, will you, Daddy?"

"You'd forget your head if it weren't attached," her father grumbled, but he went off to do her bidding.

Vivian winked at Philip. "Alone at last. Wasn't that clever of me?"

"Astoundingly brilliant," Philip replied dryly.

Vivian leaned toward him, head tilted back, eyes half-closed. Her invitation was too obvious to ignore without being rude, but rather than kiss her parted lips, Philip bussed her cheek.

Her mouth turned down in a pout. "I'm sure you can do better than that, darling."

Philip found the scent of her expensive perfume cloying and stepped back. Vivian was young, exceptionally pretty and wealthy, yet he felt nothing but mild irritation toward her now. When he'd first met her she'd seemed so enchanting, and he'd taken her to dinner a few times, only to discover the shallowness of her charm. He expected more than that in a woman now. Or rather, he *needed* more than that.

"And I'm sure you can do better than me, Vivian," he told her.

"Such modesty." Her smile was strained. "Is that what's stopped you from calling me again, Philip? Somehow I doubt it."

"I've been completely involved in this building project," he replied. He didn't want to lead her on, but he didn't want to hurt her feelings, either. And he was modest enough to be surprised at her determination to rekindle his brief interest in her. She'd been giving him languishing looks all evening.

"Oh, yes. Your project," she said. "I was fascinated with what you had to say about it tonight, Philip. I don't think my father appreciates the full scope of your new venture, though. But if you fill me in on more details..." She leaned close to him again. "Say over dinner *alone* some night soon...I'll be sure to pass along the information to Daddy. He's always interested in my recommendations."

Philip smiled. He couldn't imagine anyone, even a doting father such as Giles Grant, taking business advice from the likes of Vivian. And even if that were the case, he couldn't imagine himself using her to get to her old man. By suggesting it, Vivian had once again disappointed him. Not only had she shown little regard for his principles, but also little regard for herself.

"The last thing I want to discuss over dinner with you is business," he told her.

She slid her hand down the lapel of his jacket. "That's fine with me, too, darling. We can talk about more personal matters."

Grant came stomping back to the foyer. "Well, I couldn't find your purse anywhere, Vivian. I even looked under the table."

"Silly me! I just remembered that I didn't bring one this evening." She lowered her little chin and raised her big eyes to demonstrate her chagrin. "I'm sorry I sent you on a wild-goose chase, Dad."

"That's all right, dear. It wasn't intentional." Grant gave Philip a sharp look. "Interesting evening, Phil. But frankly I wish you were proceeding with another luxury condo project instead of the one you have in mind. Investment profits would be guaranteed then."

"Nothing ventured, nothing gained, Daddy," Vivian piped up. She winked at Philip again.

"Nothing ventured, nothing lost, either," her father said.

Philip didn't pursue the subject. It was neither the time nor the place to press Grant about backing his project. He'd accomplished what he'd set out to do, which was to plant a seed of interest. He would send Grant a detailed prospectus in the morning. He shook the financier's hand, gave Vivian another kiss on the cheek and closed the front door with great relief. Then he went to the dining room to thank the caterer, who was supervising the clean-up, for a flawless dinner. After tipping her well-trained staff, he escaped to his tower retreat.

"What a boring evening," he told King Kong, who commiserated by fetching his ball and dropping it at Philip's feet.

Philip abstractedly tossed it across the room a few times to appease the dog, wondering if it was too late to call the woman who'd been on his mind all evening, all day. He checked his watch. It was a little past eleven. She was probably in bed. He imagined the way her long lashes would fan across her high cheekbones as she slept, how her glossy cap of dark hair would look against a pale pillowcase. Did she sleep on her side? Or on her stomach? He mentally turned her over, and she smiled in her sleep, tucking the sheet beneath her chin. And as he was imagining all this, Philip was also picturing himself beside her in bed, watching over her. Yes, he thought, he would like to make Holly smile in her sleep.

Philip checked his watch again. It was still a little past eleven. Not an ungodly hour, he told himself. Maybe she was a night owl like him. Maybe, at this very moment, she was hoping he would call. Philip untied the bow of his black silk tie, unbuttoned the collar of his starched pleated shirt and reached for the telephone.

Holly had just closed her eyes when the phone by her bed rang. She groped for it in the dark, knocking the Goddess of Joy off the bed stand in the process. Crying out with dismay, she snapped on the table lamp and got out of bed to pick it up off the floor. A close examination assured her that the fall hadn't harmed it. As she pressed the goddess to her cheek with relief, she knew, instinctively, who was calling.

"Hello, Philip," she answered without thinking.

He laughed, surprised. "You must be psychic, Holly. Either that or you were dreaming about me just now. Did I wake you?"

His voice warmed her to the very core. "No, I hadn't fallen asleep yet. But when I do, maybe I *will* dream about you." She was amazed at the sound of her own voice. It had a flirtatious lilt to it. She hadn't flirted in years!

"There's something I've been wondering about, Holly," he said. "Do you prefer sleeping on your back or your stomach or your side?"

"Well, I like a variety of positions in bed," she said, then felt the heat rise to her face. She couldn't believe she'd just said that!

"I'll keep that in mind," Philip promised her.

The conversation was quickly getting out of hand, Holly decided. "Are you taking a survey of sleeping patterns, Philip? Is that why you called?"

"Actually, I called to tell you how much I enjoyed being with you last night."

"As I recall, the evening ended a bit awkwardly." Holly put the netsuke on the table. "I shouldn't have rushed off like that, and I apologize."

"I'll never take anything from you that you don't want to give me, Holly. And I'm not talking only about the goddess."

"I may not have anything else to give you," she warned him.

"I think we may have a lot to give each other," he replied. "I want to see you again, Holly."

She stared at the goddess glowing under the lamplight for a long moment. "I want to see you, too," she finally said. This admission filled her with both delight and apprehension. "But let's take things slowly, Philip. As you've probably guessed, I'm a little rusty when it comes to mating." Oh, Lord! How had that slipped out? "*Dating!* I meant dating."

He chuckled softly. "Of course you did. Do you like pizza?"

"Who doesn't?" she managed, thankful that he couldn't see the way her face had flushed.

"There's a great place in New Haven called Pepe's. Ever been there?"

"Oh, sure. It's not too far from Jerome Academy."

"Would you like to have an early dinner there with me tomorrow? Around six?"

"That would be perfect. I have student conferences until five-thirty, so I'll go straight to the restaurant from school." She hurriedly said goodbye before Philip could suggest meeting her at the academy. Her students were far too curious about her relationship with him as it was.

Chapter Six

Holly arrived at Pepe's a little after six. She didn't spot Philip and claimed a booth for them. A waiter handed her a menu. She couldn't concentrate on it. She was much too busy keeping an eye on the entrance. Her heart stopped each time the door opened, then plunged with disappointment. Over and over again. At six-thirty she made up her mind to leave if Philip didn't show up in five minutes.

Five minutes later she was still sitting there alone as the restaurant filled. Her booth was like a little island of isolation as cheery families and laughing couples took seats around her. Five more minutes and that's it, she decided.

The waiter delivered a pizza to a party who had arrived long after she had. Holly shifted uncomfortably when he glanced her way. She knew he wanted her to either order something or leave. She'd used up the five additional minutes her waning pride had allowed her. She could hear an echo in her ear. *Give up hoping, you fool, and go now!*

Philip came through the door at that moment. He caught sight of Holly immediately, and they locked eyes across the room. The rest of the world fell away at that moment, and only they existed. But just for a moment. In the next Holly noticed that he wasn't alone. There was a boy with him.

Philip crossed the restaurant with long strides, the boy following him. "I'm sorry I'm late," he said when he reached the table. "I had to pick up Snake here."

"Snake?" Holly smiled at the thin, dark-haired boy. He couldn't have been more than ten. "Why are you called that?"

"What's it to you, lady?" the boy snarled.

Philip placed a firm hand on his shoulder. "Hey, easy, pal. Don't be rude to Mrs. Murphey. You got that straight?"

The boy twisted his frail shoulder away from Philip's hand and readjusted the shape of his black leather jacket, which was about three sizes too large for him. "Yeah, I got it."

"Now go wash your hands."

"What?" The boy gave Philip a defiant look.

"If you're going to share a pizza with us, the first rule is to have clean hands."

"You like making rules, don't you, mister? You like playing the big boss."

"Hey, I'm not playing at it, Snake. As long as you're with me, I *am* the boss. You got that straight, too?"

"Yeah, I got it."

"Now go wash your hands."

The conversation had come full circle, and Holly wondered if it would go around and around and around. But Snake surprised her by turning away, thin little back ramrod straight, and marching off to the men's room.

"I suppose you're wondering who that delightful child is," Philip said, sliding into the booth opposite Holly. His long legs brushed against hers as he stretched them out.

"Let me guess. He's our chaperon."

Philip, grinning, put his elbows on the table and leaned closer to her. "The last thing I want between us is a chaperon, lovely lady." His knees pressed against hers under the table.

Holly leaned closer, too, and pressed back, enjoying the intimacy of their secret contact. "Then who is he?" she asked, her voice huskier than usual.

"The son of one of the guys on my construction crew." His eyes glittered as he took in her face. "Have you become more beautiful since Saturday? I don't know how that's possible, but you have, Holly."

"It must be the restaurant lighting," she said.

"Or the light in your eyes when you look at me."

"You really are such an egotist, Philip."

"No. I'm an optimist. I have my hopes set on you falling in love with me."

Holly considered his comment too cavalier and shifted her legs, breaking contact with his. She shifted the tone of the conversation, too. "I still don't understand why you brought along the boy."

Philip leaned back in the booth. "The police came and arrested his father at one of my building sites late this afternoon. When I found out about it, I went to the station to see what I could do for him."

"Why was he arrested?"

"Hit and run. Don't look so horrified. It was a parked car—no one was hurt. Johnson claims he didn't do it. I'll pay his bail once it's set and get him a lawyer."

"Do you think he's innocent?" Holly asked.

Philip shrugged. "I have no idea. Johnson just started working for me a few weeks ago. I barely know him. But he's my employee, so I feel a certain responsibility. When he asked me to look after his kid until he got out of jail, I couldn't refuse."

"What about the boy's mother?"

"Johnson says she split, and he doesn't know where she is now."

Holly's heart squeezed tight. "Poor boy."

Philip nodded, his expression grim. "He looked so small and scared when I told him about his father. They live in this cheap roominghouse in a pretty bad section of New Haven. There were spaced-out freaks hanging around the front stoop when I went to pick Snake up."

"Thank God the boy didn't have to spend the night alone there." Holly placed her hand over Philip's and felt the warmth and strength of it. "He's fortunate that you got involved."

"He's not the friendliest kid I've ever encountered."

"He's upset about his father. And we're complete strangers to him. Maybe he'll let down his defenses once he feels more comfortable with us."

Philip sighed. "It's hardly the romantic evening I had planned for us."

"Oh?" Holly arched her dark, sleek eyebrows. "Was romance on your agenda?"

Philip pressed his legs against hers again. "Sure. Didn't you know that Pepe's famous white pizza is an aphrodisiac?"

"With all that garlic?" Holly laughed. "I doubt it."

"*White* pizza? Yuk!" Snake had returned.

"Welcome back," Philip said, pushing as much enthusiasm as he could into his voice. "Take a seat, pal."

The boy chose to sit next to Philip rather than Holly. But he apparently didn't want Philip to view this as a friendly gesture. "I'm not your pal," he stated emphatically.

"Maybe we'll become pals. Who knows?" Philip replied.

The boy narrowed his eyes at that unlikely possibility. "And I ain't eating no white pizza, neither. What did you call it? An Afro dizzy act?"

"It's a garlic and clam pie," Holly hurriedly explained, not quite answering his question. "But we'll order a tomato pizza instead. What would you like on it?"

He lifted his shoulders.

"Mushrooms?" Holly asked. The boy wrinkled his nose. "Sausage?" He wrinkled his whole face. "Onions? Pepperoni? Meatballs?" The boy's thin face became more and more contorted with each suggestion Holly made. She gave up. "How about a plain pizza?"

Snake rewarded her suggestion with a curt nod of approval but avoided meeting her eyes.

It turned out that the boy, despite his small size, had a tremendous appetite, and Philip ordered another pizza for Holly and himself as soon as he saw how quickly Snake was wolfing down the first one. Along with his voraciousness, Snake displayed a total disregard for table manners. He hunched over the table, balanced on his elbows, chewed with his mouth open, slurped his soda, licked his fingers rather than deign to use a napkin and belched with a great deal of enthusiasm.

Poor, motherless boy, Holly thought. "When's the last time you ate?" she asked him gently.

"I dunno. I don't remember."

"You had lunch at school, didn't you?"

He threw down his pizza crust. "What is this, lady? The third degree?"

Philip threw down his crust, too. "Hey, now listen—"

Holly gave him a little kick under the table, then met his surprised look with a plea in her eyes. She didn't want him to reprimand the boy. What good would it do? "How would you like a nice salad now?" she asked Snake. There was no doubt in her mind that he lacked vegetables in his diet.

"A nice salad?" he repeated, mimicking her with a high-pitched, prissy voice, then laughing harshly. "Give me a break, will ya, lady?"

Again Holly caught Philip's angry eyes with a plea in hers and shook her head. She didn't really mind Snake's rudeness. When it came to children, she had a high level of tolerance. She turned her attention to the boy. "You don't have to call me lady. Or Mrs. Murphey, either. Call me Holly," she said.

He regarded her suspiciously. "Are you a social worker or something?"

"No, I'm not a social worker, Snake."

"What are you then?"

Holly considered lying for a brief moment—telling him she was a female wrestler or a race-car driver or a karate expert. Instead she bit the bullet and told the truth. "I'm a high-school English teacher."

Her reply got just the reaction she'd expected it would from the recalcitrant Snake. He squished up his narrow little face again. "A *teacher*!" He made a very unpleasant gagging sound.

"That's enough," Philip said. "I've had it with you, kid. Now that you've eaten, go wait in the car. I'll be there in a few minutes."

Snake obeyed immediately, which surprised Holly. Then again, she could well imagine how impressive a big, rugged man such as Philip must be to a ten-year-old boy. He was pretty impressive to a thirty-three-year-old woman, too, she had to admit.

"Maybe you shouldn't let him go off on his own, Philip," she cautioned.

He swiveled in the booth and watched the little boy in the oversized leather jacket swagger out. "You're right," he said, getting up. "I'll make sure the little monster really does go to the car, then I'll be right back."

"I don't think it's wise to leave him alone," she said. "Why don't we call it a night." She made a move to stand up.

"No, please, Holly. Wait." His big palm gently pressed on her shoulder before she could rise. "I wouldn't leave Snake alone. The limo's parked right out front, and my driver will take care of him for a while. Sit tight."

His driver? Holly marveled. His limo? But why should that surprise her? She'd already seen where Philip lived. A man who had a showplace mansion would most likely have a limousine and driver. Her eyes followed him as he hurried toward the restaurant door. She smiled, taking in his faded Lee jeans and shabby corduroy jacket. Philip certainly didn't advertise his wealth with his clothes.

That fact went into the ever-increasing plus column she'd been mentally adding to since she'd met him. There was also a minus column, but it was much shorter. She'd only listed two things on the minus side of her Philip Irons tally. One, he wanted her goddess. Two, he excited her. Perhaps the second could have as easily gone in the plus column, but it made her wary of him. For a man she didn't know well, he excited her way too much.

His wealth also made her wary of him. Why would Philip Irons be interested in a simple schoolteacher? Apparently money hadn't made him feel above the simple pleasures in life, though, such as eating lunch in the park on a lovely spring day, or owning a mutt, or having pizza at Pepe's.

Philip returned and slid into the booth beside Holly. His masculine bulk seemed to fill all available space, and she felt a vibrating thrill as his body pressed against hers.

"Alone at last," he said. He tilted up her chin with his index finger and kissed her briefly on the lips. "I've been dying to do that all evening."

Holly licked her bottom lip, tasting him.

"If you do that again, you'll drive me crazy," Philip said. "You don't want me to go crazy in a public restaurant, do you?"

"It would be a little embarrassing," Holly said, but she licked her bottom lip again anyway.

"I warned you." Philip dipped his face and kissed her with more passion. Her mouth softened beneath the pressure of his, and she could feel her very marrow softening. She drew away from him slowly but with firm resolution.

"Snake's waiting for you," she reminded him.

Philip groaned. "I promised I'd take him bowling now."

"What? On a school night?"

"I didn't even think of that. But it's still early. Why don't you come with us?"

"Me?" Holly laughed at the idea.

"Please," Philip urged. "You can handle the little urchin better than I can. You're more patient with him."

Holly considered for a moment. She felt sorry for the boy, and she really didn't want to say good-night to Philip. "All right," she agreed. "But I haven't bowled in years."

"Neither have I," Philip said. "Since high school. I really appreciate this, sweetheart." He planted a kiss on her forehead.

Warmth flowed from her crown to the tips of her toes. She liked being called sweetheart by Philip. She liked it very much.

When Philip's limousine pulled up in front of the Bowl-A-Rama just outside New Haven, people in the parking lot turned and pointed. Holly felt a little self-conscious, sure they were expecting some celebrity to emerge from the car. Snake played it up to the hilt, though. He put on a pair of cheap sunglasses, which he pulled out of the pocket of his jacket, turned up the collar and strutted and danced toward the entrance with the flamboyance of Michael Jackson. Holly and Philip, following, smiled at each other.

After renting bowling shoes, they went to their assigned lane and sat together on a plastic bench to put them on. The boy protested about the "geeky" shoes, but when Philip gave him the choice of either wearing them or going back to the car, he relented.

"Too bad your driver wouldn't join us," Holly said.

"I was pretty sure he'd refuse when I asked him," Philip replied. "Jack usually prefers to read in the car or listen to his collection of tapes while he's waiting for me."

"I thought you told me that you didn't like people at your beck and call," Holly couldn't help but remark.

"I don't. It took me a long time to get used to having someone drive me around. But with a tight schedule like mine, it's a necessary indulgence." He grinned. "Besides, it impresses people."

Holly sniffed. "Not everyone."

"You kidding, lady?" the boy asked. He was still wearing his sunglasses. "Didn't you see how everyone stared at us when we got out?"

"Only at you, Snake," Philip said, still grinning. "You stole the show with that moon-walking bit of yours."

"Yeah?" He smiled for the first time all evening. "I was pretty good, huh?"

"You were great," Holly assured him. "How'd you learn all those fancy dance steps?"

"My dad taught me. He used to play lead guitar in a band when we lived in—" The boy stopped himself.

"Lived where?" Philip asked.

"I don't remember." He pushed up his sunglasses. "How long they gonna keep my dad in jail?"

"They'll probably post bail and release him tomorrow," Philip told him. He reached across the plastic bench and patted the boy's back. "Don't worry, Snake. I got him a good lawyer."

"Who said I was worried?" The boy's expression remained blank behind his dark glasses. But a tear slid from behind them. He yanked off the glasses and swiped at his eyes. "Hey, are we gonna bowl, or what?"

He sprang from the bench, grabbed a ball and rolled it down the alley. Or rather, down the gutter. Then another and another. He turned back to them with a sullen face.

"This ain't no fun. Let's get outta here," he said.

Holly got up and joined him. "Sure it's fun," she said. "Once you get the hang of it."

"And I suppose you're gonna show me how to do it, lady."

"That's right, Snake. At least I'm going to attempt to."

He gave a derisive laugh. Holly slipped her fingers into a ball, felt the familiar weight of it in her hands, took a deep breath and went into the smooth motions she'd practised so many Saturday mornings as a girl. The moment she released the ball, she experienced that special exhilaration once again. It had been a clean release with a good follow-through, and she raised her arms in triumph before the ball even touched the pins. Muscle memory told her that she'd thrown a strike.

And she had. Philip applauded as all the pins rattled down. "Poetry in motion," he shouted.

"Not bad," the boy reluctantly admitted. "But I bet you can't do it again."

"You're tough to impress, aren't you, Snake?"

"You just got lucky," he said.

Holly waited for the pins to be reset and took up another ball. She doubted she could do it again. But she was willing to give it a try.

She turned to look at Philip. He beamed encouragement. And as pins crashed and people yelled all around her, there was a sudden quiet within Holly as she basked in the bright beam Philip directed at her. She turned, glided up the runway and released another perfect ball. Please carry, she whispered. It did, curving just right. Another strike.

Even Snake applauded this time. "Not bad for a girl," he said.

She laughed and ruffled his dark hair. It was soft as puppy fur. Surprisingly, he didn't draw back.

"Okay," he said. "Teach me how to do that."

He never quite got the hang of it, but it didn't matter. The three of them ended up having a good time. Philip, a natural athlete, turned out to be a natural comedian, too, making Holly and the boy howl with laughter as he used outlandish body language to direct his balls. Holly adored watching him move. He had a masculine grace that stemmed from a confidence in his rugged body, and she found him compellingly sexy even when he was clowning.

After an hour or so, Snake declared that he was hungry.

"What are you, pal? A bottomless pit?" Philip joked. "What would you like to eat? Ice cream?"

"I wouldn't spit on it," the boy replied.

Not the most gracious reply, Holly thought, but at least he didn't snarl when Philip addressed him as pal.

"What about you, Holly?" Philip asked. "Would you spit on it?"

"Not if it's vanilla," she assured him.

They went to the Bowl-A-Rama restaurant, which was as bright and shiny as the bowling lanes and almost as noisy. Snake showed a considerable improvement in his table manners as he ate his hot-fudge sundae and even offered a bite of it to Holly and Philip. They both took a spoonful.

"I bet people at the other tables think we're a family," the boy said, looking around and smiling.

Holly and Philip exchanged glances.

"I always wanted to go bowling with my mom and dad, but we never got around to it," Snake continued. "They used to take me to basketball games, though. Mom always asked a lot of dumb questions about what was going on. It drove Dad crazy, but I didn't mind." The boy smiled indulgently. "Just so she rooted for the home team."

"Which team was that?" Philip asked casually.

"The Seventy-sixers, man!"

Philip nodded. "So you come from Philadelphia."

The boy shifted uncomfortably. "I never *said* that. My dad doesn't like me telling people where we're from."

"Why not, honey?" Holly looked at him closely.

He gave her a beseeching look in return. "Don't ask me any more questions, okay?"

"All right," Holly acquiesced. She didn't want Snake to shut them out just when he was beginning to trust them. She glanced at Philip and could see that he was thinking the same thing.

They made an attempt to converse with Snake about the neutral subject of sports, but he'd stopped being communicative. After he'd played with his sundae a while and it became obvious that he wasn't going to finish it, they left the restaurant.

The boy sat between Holly and Philip in the car. As they traveled to New Haven to drop Holly off at her apartment, he leaned his head against her shoulder.

"You smell real good, Holly," he said. "Like my mom."

Holly had to bite the inside of her mouth to keep back the tears. She reached for his bony little hand and held it in her lap. His breathing became deep and regular.

"He's fallen asleep," she whispered to Philip.

"I know. I've been watching the two of you."

She turned her head slightly to look at him. He was smiling softly as he gazed at her and the sleeping boy.

When the car stopped in front of Holly's three-family apartment house, Snake woke up. He looked around like a startled fawn. "Where are we?"

"This is where I live," Holly explained softly. "Good night, honey." She gave him a kiss on the forehead.

"Wait!" he demanded. "I want to come with you. Why can't I spend the night at your place, Holly?"

"That's not the plan, Snake," Philip explained patiently. "I'm taking you to my home in Fairfield. Now sit tight while I walk Holly to her door, okay?"

"I want to walk her to the door, too," Snake insisted. He climbed over Philip and scrambled out of the car.

Philip swore under his breath and got out, too. He bowed and offered his hand to Holly. "Your two escorts await, madam."

When they reached the porch Snake jumped from one foot to the other. "I have to go to the bathroom," he said.

Philip laughed sharply. "You got a great line, kid. That's a surefire way to make a lady invite you in."

"Right this way, gentlemen," Holly said. She led them up the stairs to her second-floor apartment.

"Too bad your bathroom door doesn't lock from the outside," Philip said when Snake closed it behind him. "Then we could have a few minutes to ourselves. I think the kid has fallen in love with you, Holly." He sighed dramatically. "Not that I blame him. But I hadn't planned on having a ten-year-old rival for your affections."

She smiled sadly. "Oh, Philip, he misses his mother. That's why he's connecting with me. Why take him all the way to Fairfield when he has to come back to New Haven for school tomorrow? He can spend the night here. The sofa opens into a bed. Maybe I can get more information out of him. This mystery about where he comes from bothers me."

"Me, too. Plenty. There's something obviously wrong with the boy's situation, and I intend to look into it. But you don't have to get involved, Holly."

"I am involved. I can't help it. I feel so sorry for him."

"Yeah, so do I," Philip admitted. "Beneath that tough act he's just a frightened little boy."

"Let him stay with me tonight. I'll take him to school tomorrow and ask the principal about him."

"All right," Philip agreed. He took her into his arms. "I wish I were the one spending the night, though. Lord, how I wish that!"

He lowered his face, and she tilted hers up, tingling with excitement even before their lips met.

"You're not gonna kiss, are you?" Snake asked, returning to the living room. He made his offensive gagging sound.

Philip and Holly quickly drew apart.

"There's no doubt about it, Snake," Philip said dryly. "You're a real charmer."

Chapter Seven

French toast, orange juice and cocoa—Danny's favorite breakfast. But Holly would not allow herself to pretend, for even a short, sweet moment, that she was preparing this meal for Danny. She hadn't made French toast in years, and the only reason she was doing so now was that Snake had specifically requested it.

Snake! She couldn't stand that name, but so far he'd refused to tell her his real one. He'd refused to tell her anything. Frowning, she cracked an egg against a bowl. Why was the boy so secretive?

Snake padded into the kitchen, fresh from the shower she'd ordered him to take, a towel wrapped around his skinny torso. He left wet footprints in his wake. "Where are my clothes, Holly?"

"I washed them. They're in the dryer now."

"Everything? Even my underwear?"

"Especially your underwear!"

"Holly, you didn't throw my leather jacket in the washing machine, did you?" His eyes widened with apprehension.

"No, I burned that." She smiled at his horrified expression. "Just joking, honey. I didn't touch your jacket." She would have liked to have burned it, though. "I left one of my sweat suits in the living room for you. You can wear that while you eat breakfast."

"Okay," he said, surprisingly agreeable. He padded off to the living room to dress.

When he returned, Holly was dunking bread in the egg and milk mixture. He leaned over the counter and intently observed the procedure. "My mom doesn't do it like that," he finally announced. "She puts the bread in a dish and then pours the eggy stuff over it."

"Each master chef has her own method," Holly replied lightly, trying not to let on how interested she was in hearing about his mother. "When's the last time your mom made breakfast for you, honey?"

"The day she left."

"And how long ago was that?"

His narrow face closed. "Why do you care?"

"Because I like you. I want to know all about you."

"How come you don't have kids?" he asked, using one of her favorite tricks of deflecting questions with questions.

Holly's own face closed. "I just don't."

"Does Phil have kids?"

"No."

Snake considered this information for a moment. "Maybe you could give each other some," he suggested.

Every muscle in Holly's body tightened. "Oh, dear. The butter's going to burn if I don't hurry," she said. She turned away from the boy and placed the soaking bread in the sizzling skillet.

She served Snake at the kitchen table and checked the stove clock. "It's six-thirty. What time did you have to be at school?"

"Eight-thirty," Snake said around a huge mouthful.

"That late? I thought elementary school started at eight."

Snake gulped down the food in his mouth. "Yeah. That's what I meant."

"Well, we have plenty of time." Holly, still in her robe, poured herself some coffee. She joined Snake at the table and watched him wolf down his breakfast.

What could be more enjoyable, she mused, than watching a hungry child eat food she had prepared? How Danny enjoyed eating—no! She stopped herself short before taking that train of thought. She could control her thoughts about her son now. She could control them even when there was another boy the same age Danny would have been sitting across the table from her. She'd become strong enough to do that, she assured herself.

Snake swirled the last forkful of toast in the maple syrup coating his plate and shoved the dripping morsel into his mouth. He washed it down with a big slurp of orange juice.

"Better not drink your cocoa as fast," Holly warned. "You don't want to burn your tongue."

"Hey, I know that. Don't treat me like some baby. I'm almost eleven."

"Sorry. I guess I don't know how to treat boys your age."

"That's okay," Snake allowed forgivingly. "How could you know, not having one yourself."

Holly sipped her coffee and said nothing.

"That was a pretty good breakfast," Snake told her.

"Why, thank you." She couldn't have been more pleased if a great chef had complimented her culinary talents.

"Did you really mean it when you said you liked me?" Snake asked her.

"Yes, of course I did." Holly reached across the table and ruffled the boy's hair, still damp from his shower.

"I like it when you do that," he said. "You're nice, Holly. Phil is, too. He made me laugh last night when we went bowling."

"He was pretty funny, all right." Holly smiled into her coffee cup.

"You should have invited him to sleep over, too, Holly. It would have been fun."

The boy had innocently conjured up some very disturbing images for Holly. She placed her cup in the saucer with a sharp click. "I'd better get dressed for work, Snake. I have to drop you off at school first."

"No, you don't," he quickly told her. "I can walk there from here. It's just around the corner."

Holly looked at him sharply. "There's no school in this neighborhood."

"No? I must have gotten mixed up about where I was last night."

"What's the name of your school, Snake?"

"Uh... I forget." He caught Holly's frown. "Oh, yeah. I just remembered. Lincoln Elementary. That's it."

"Do you remember the street?"

He shook his head, looking miserable.

"Don't worry," Holly said. "I'll look it up and get you there on time."

Her assurance made him look all the more anxious. "I always go to school alone, Holly. I'd look like a geek if you came with me. I'm too big for that."

"But you're in a different neighborhood, honey. You might get lost."

"I don't feel so good," he said, clutching his stomach.

He did look suddenly very pale to Holly. She reached across the table again, automatically, to touch his forehead. "You don't seem to have a fever. Is it your stomach that hurts?"

He nodded. "I better not go to school today."

Holly smiled to herself. Had Snake pegged her for a pushover? But he really did look ill. "Maybe you ate breakfast too fast, honey. Go lie down while I take a quick shower and get dressed. Then we'll see how you feel."

Still clutching his stomach, Snake left the table and threw himself on the sofa bed in the living room. Holly turned on the TV for him.

"I think *Mister Rogers* is on at this time," she said, remembering how Danny had loved that show.

"*Mister Rogers*!" Snake's tone was disdainful. "I stopped watching that kiddy show years and years ago, Holly."

"Of course. I keep forgetting how old you are." She handed him the remote-control unit. "Choose whatever you'd like," she said and went to take her shower.

As Holly shampooed her hair, it hit her. Snake didn't go to school! She quickly rinsed her hair, shut off the shower and dried herself. Slipping on her terrycloth robe and belting it tightly, she marched to the living room, determined to get the whole truth from him.

The boy was sprawled on the bed, laughing at a cartoon show, eating a jelly doughnut. A jelly doughnut? Holly stopped in her tracks, stunned. How in the world did he get a hold of a jelly...

"Good morning, Holly." Philip came out of the kitchen holding a cup of coffee. "When Snake let me in he said you were taking a shower so I helped myself to some coffee. Hope you don't mind."

She looked at him, too stunned to speak for a moment. Would the sight of him always affect her this way? she wondered. Her heart pounded, and she felt a rush through her system. He looked so good to her, dressed in a superbly tailored gray business suit and conservative red tie. But he always looked good to her, no matter what he was wearing. His vibrancy seemed to encompass the whole apartment.

She combed her fingers through her wet hair, attempting to fluff it up a bit. Did she look simply awful? she worried. She hadn't glanced in a mirror all morning. But then she looked into Philip's eyes and didn't need a mirror. His expression reflected total pleasure at the sight of her.

Holly in the morning, Philip thought. This was the sight he wanted to wake up to. He liked the way her wet, slicked-back hair made her look like as sleek as a seal. Her blue eyes looked so bright beneath the high expanse of her smooth forehead. And her mouth, half open in surprise—he wanted to nibble at the full bottom lip. His eyes skidded down her figure to her pretty bare feet, and he couldn't help but wonder if she were naked beneath her robe. If they were alone, he would have done his best to find out. But they weren't alone, dammit!

"I can't stay long," Philip said. "I've got a big board meeting scheduled. But I dropped by to check how you and Snake were getting along first. I brought doughnuts."

"Yes, so I noticed." She glanced at Snake stuffing his face, eyes glued to the TV screen, then motioned Philip toward the kitchen.

Philip followed Holly in through the swinging door. He put his cup on the counter and reached for her. "Come here," he demanded, silver eyes flashing with intensity.

He was like a magnet to her, and she stepped into his arms. The moment they touched, currents of desire shot threw Holly, and she threw back her head, offering him her lips. They kissed with breathless urgency, as if they would never have the chance to kiss again. Holly pressed closer to him, and he moaned, molding her body with his palms through the soft terry cloth. His touch was bold, persuasive, and her body softened as she clung to him. Her legs grew weak beneath her, and she wanted to slide to the floor, pulling him down with her. But that was insanity. She twisted away from him, using every ounce of her willpower.

"Snake," she whispered. "He could walk in on us at any moment." She leaned against the refrigerator, still dizzy from his kiss, and looked at Philip with longing and regret.

Philip took a few steadying breaths before he spoke. "Please don't look at me like that, sweetheart," he begged, his voice even deeper than usual. "It's hard enough to keep my hands off you right now."

She averted her face, placing her flushed cheek against the cool surface of the refrigerator door. It helped her regain her equilibrium.

"I just realized what Snake is," Philip said. "He's a *baku*!"

"A what?" Holly shook her head. Then she remembered the netsuke Philip had showed her and smiled. "You mean that mischievous creature who comes into your life and bedevils you?"

"That sounds like Snake, all right, doesn't it?" He leaned closer to her, and Holly breathed in his scent, a combination of soap, light, tangy after-shave, starch from his dress shirt and natural masculine musk. "I have a plan," he said in a conspiratorial tone.

Holly released her breath with a quivering little sigh. "A plan?"

"To make Snake disappear. I'll go in and bow to him, and he'll bow back, because *baku* are supremely polite . . ." Philip sighed deeply. "I guess that doesn't sound like Snake after all. He's pesky enough, but he sure isn't polite."

"Actually, he's been rather sweet this morning. Incommunicative but sweet. I'm glad you came by. I need to talk to you about him."

"That's not what *I* need right now." Philip played with the knot of her belt. "I couldn't stop thinking about you all night, sweetheart. Would you like to hear about all the wonderful things I was imagining us doing together?"

His deep voice was soft, arousing, and Holly nodded. She was all ears. But before Philip could tell her more, Snake pushed through the swinging door.

"Holly, I'm thirsty," he whined. "Can I have some milk to wash down the doughnuts?"

"The *baku* strikes again," Philip murmured, dropping his hand from Holly's belt.

"I'm glad you recovered from your stomachache, Snake," Holly said, opening the refrigerator and taking out a carton of milk. "Now you can go to school."

"No, my stomach still hurts," the boy insisted. "Even worse now. I shouldn't have had all those doughnuts." He clutched at his middle and doubled up, groaning.

"Poor thing," Holly said sweetly, pouring him a glass of milk. "Here, drink this, honey. It'll make you feel better."

Snake took the glass, threw back his skinny neck and drained the glass. "Nope," he reported after a little burp. "I still feel real sick."

"You don't look sick to me, pal," Philip said.

"Oh, I think he does," Holly countered. "I think Snake should stay in bed and watch cartoons all day."

Philip gave her a quizzical look. Snake gave her an approving smile.

"Of course I'll have to call your school, Snake, and tell them you won't be coming in today."

His smile quickly faded. "You don't have to do that, Holly. Just give me a note for tomorrow, and everything will be fine."

"Oh, no. Your teacher will be worried if you don't show up today. I'll call information and get the number." She picked up the kitchen phone, her eyes never leaving his face. "What's the name of your school? Lincoln Elementary?"

"Maybe that was the name of the last one I went to."

Holly hung up the phone. "You're not enrolled in any school now, are you, honey?"

He shook his head.

"You don't go to school?" Philip stared at him hard.

"Not since we came to New Haven, I haven't."

"How long ago was that?" Holly asked him.

Snake shrugged his thin shoulders. "Since Mom left me." He turned to Philip. "When are they going to let my dad out of jail?"

"I don't know yet, pal. The lawyer will call me as soon as he hears."

"Will Dad get into more trouble about not sending me to school? I wasn't supposed to tell anybody about that."

"It's okay that you did," Philip assured the boy. "But why didn't he send you to school, Snake?"

"Dad says we're not gonna stay around here for long. We're going to travel all over the place, he says."

Shaking her head, Holly picked up the milk carton, intending to put it back in the refrigerator. She noticed the picture of the missing child printed on the back of the carton, and her blood ran cold. But she forced a smile. "Honey, can I talk to Philip alone for a little bit longer?"

"You want to kiss him, don't you?" He rolled his eyes and went to the living room.

"You want to kiss me, don't you?" Philip said, imitating Snake's disparaging tone. "Well, all right. I'll let you if you don't get too mushy about it."

Holly was in no mood for joking—or kissing—now. "Philip, take a look at this," she demanded. Her hand trembled as she pointed to the picture on the milk carton.

He studied it carefully. "Holly, this picture doesn't look a bit like Snake. And the description doesn't fit."

"I know. But I think Snake's a missing child, too."

"You mean Johnson kidnapped him?"

"It's possible." She shivered. "Maybe Johnson isn't even his father."

Philip frowned and shook his head. "That doesn't add up, Holly. Snake would have told us he wasn't by now. He would have asked for our help."

"Unless he's too frightened to. Johnson could have made all kinds of horrible threats to him." Holly shivered again.

Philip wrapped his arms around her. "Take it easy, sweetheart. The simple explanation could be that Johnson is just an irresponsible jerk who doesn't give a damn if his kid goes to school or not. Snake keeps referring to him as his dad, and he's also backed up Johnson's claim that the mother took off."

"No, I can't believe that a mother would desert her child."

"It happens, Holly."

"Rarely, though. And whenever Snake talks about his mom, it's with such warmth. He told me that she makes French toast for him."

"That hardly qualifies her for the mother of the year award."

"We have to locate her, Philip." She drew back from his arms to look at him. "We can't let Snake go back to Johnson until we talk to his mother."

"All right," Philip agreed softly. "We'll do our best to track her down. Let's start by asking Snake a few more questions."

"Gently, though. If we upset him, he won't tell us anything."

"I can be very gentle," Philip assured her.

Holly believed him with all her heart as a warm glow suffused her. "Why don't you go try your luck with him while I get dressed," she suggested.

His hand strayed to the belt on her robe again. "I'd much rather help you out of this bulky thing. You're not wearing anything under it, are you?"

Her lips tilted up, but she stepped back. "Now isn't a good time to find out, Philip," she reminded him.

"Would you let me find out if we were alone?" He stared at her intently.

She broke his gaze. "There's no point to this discussion, Philip, because we're not alone."

"Not now. But we will be eventually, Holly. Snake isn't going to be with us forever. So you think long and hard about your answer, okay?" He kissed her quickly and left.

Holly watched the door swing and took a deep breath. Alone with Philip...she could dwell on the possibilities for hours. Her eyes drifted to the milk carton on the counter. No, she couldn't. Not now. She couldn't think about anything until she got to the heart of Snake's secret. She had to somehow locate his mother and find out the truth. She reached for the wall phone and called the academy to say she wasn't coming in. She'd never missed a day since she'd started teaching there, and she felt guilty about doing so now. But she would have felt even more guilty if she'd left Snake. Ms. Salverone told Holly that she would take over her classes for her. Holly thanked her, then went to her bedroom to change into one of her simple dark dresses.

When she joined Philip and Snake in the living room, they were sitting on the edge of the sofa bed, watching a Popeye cartoon. Philip was laughing even harder than the boy.

"I see you've used this time alone with Snake constructively," Holly said, but she couldn't help but smile. She adored Philip's laugh. It was deep and husky, more like a chortle. A contagious laugh.

"Snake's not in a very talkative mood, so I told him he could watch one more cartoon." Philip patted the space between himself and Snake. "Sit down, Holly. This is the best part, where Popeye gets his spinach fix and saves Olive Oyl."

Not wanting to be a spoilsport, she complied. Philip took her hand and absently rubbed his thumb against her palm.

Holly relaxed, enjoying the traveling caress of his thumb up and down her palm's sensitive life line, and began laughing along with the man and boy sitting on either side of her. Her contralto blended in with Philip's baritone chuckle and Snake's giggling soprano. She felt a familiar warmth envelop her. She'd been part of a scene very similar to this many times before. No! She couldn't let herself expect or even wish for that kind of happiness again. As soon as the cartoon ended, she snapped off the TV.

"Please. Just one more," Snake pleaded.

"No, Holly's right. Show time's over," Philip said. "Now it's talk time. We want you to help us find your mom, pal."

"She's *gone*!" the boy shouted. "And Dad says she's never coming back."

"Why don't we try calling her?" Holly suggested. "At your old phone number in Philadelphia. Do you remember it?"

"Of course I remember it. I even know how to dial it long distance. But every time I do, a strange lady answers. When I ask her where my mom is she won't answer, then she hangs up."

Philip's eyes flashed with anger. "What's the number, Snake? Let *me* deal with that heartless—" He stopped himself. "With that woman."

Snake recited the number, and Philip went to the kitchen to call, his ruddy face set with determination.

"I'm sure Philip will persuade this woman to give us information about your mother's whereabouts," Holly told Snake.

The boy looked doubtful. "I don't think she even knows my mom, Holly."

Philip returned a minute later. "Dead end," he announced.

"You couldn't get anything out of that woman?" Holly asked, disappointed that he'd given up so quickly.

"You can't get much information out of a recording, Holly. The chirpy female voice on the other end informed me that the number's been disconnected."

Snake nodded. "Yeah, that's what she kept telling me, too. So I finally gave up calling." There was a little catch in his voice.

Holly sat beside him and took his hand. "Honey, do you have any grandparents?"

"Sure I do. But I don't remember their number. They live in Chicago."

"What are their names?"

He looked at her as if she'd asked something stupid. "Grandma and Grandpa."

Holly smiled. "Their last name, honey. Do you know that?"

He thought a moment. "White."

"What's Grandpa's first name?"

Snake shifted restlessly. "I don't know. Mom calls him Pop. And Grandma calls him Grandpa."

"What do other people call him?" Holly pressed.

"Mr. White!"

"Great. Mr. White in Chicago," Philip said. "Easy as finding a needle in a haystack. What about your father's parents, Snake?"

"He doesn't have any. He always tells me how tough it was growing up. He says I'm lucky to have him now that Mom doesn't want me anymore." His thin shoulders slumped. "I really do feel kinda sick now," he complained. "And that's the truth."

"I believe you, Snake." Holly hugged him.

"Can I lay my head in your lap?"

The doors to Holly's heart flung wide open. "Yes, of course you can, honey." When he put his little head in her lap, she stroked his hair to relax him. "We won't ask you any more questions for awhile, will we, Philip."

He nodded in agreement when she looked at him, then checked his watch. "It's almost nine. I better call my office and cancel my board meeting."

"You don't have to do that," Holly said. "I'll look after Snake today."

"I'm not leaving," Philip told her. "We're in this together."

She liked the sound of that. "I have an idea," she told him. "Call the Philadelphia board of education while you're at it. Ask if there's a Lincoln Elementary School, and if there is, talk to the principal about..." She looked down at the boy.

He nodded again. "Great idea, Holly." He went to the kitchen.

When Philip returned ten minutes later Snake had fallen asleep in Holly's lap. Philip sat on the chair across from them. "There is a Lincoln Elementary," he reported in a low voice. "And the principal is very concerned about a ten-year-old boy who was reported missing by his mother. The boy fits Snake's description, but his name is Gale Fletcher. His parents are divorced, and the mother has custody. She remarried three weeks ago and left the boy in the care of his father when she went on her honeymoon. He disappeared with the child."

"Johnson?" Holly whispered.

"Most likely. But his real name is Joe Fletcher."

"Now what do we do?"

"The principal gave me the woman's number. I think you should call her to make sure she really is Snake's mother before we tell him about it."

"*You* call her, Philip." Holly didn't think she could handle discussing a lost son with his mother.

"No, it would be better if you did," Philip insisted softly. "You've spent more time with the boy than I have. You can compare notes to determine if Snake really is Gale Fletcher. Besides, if you were in that poor woman's situation, wouldn't you prefer to talk to another woman?"

"You're right." Holly couldn't fight his logic unless she bared her soul to him. And she had no intention of doing that at the moment.

"Here," Philip said, handing Holly a slip of paper. "This is the number the principal gave me. Gale Fletcher's mother. Her name is Mrs. Ferrell now."

Snake instantly awoke when Holly shifted to get up. "Where are you going, Holly?" he demanded.

"Just to my bedroom for a minute. I'll be right back."

"How about watching more cartoons?" Philip asked enthusiastically. He turned the TV volume up high.

Holly went to her bedroom and closed the door. She sank on the bed and tried to compose herself. She picked up the Goddess of Joy from her night table, and it smiled back encouragement. She dialed the number.

"Hello," a woman answered.

"Is this Mrs. Ferrell?" Holly asked.

"Yes. Who is this?"

"You don't know me, Mrs. Ferrell. I'm calling about a boy who may be your son."

"You know where Gale is?"

"This boy calls himself Snake."

"Yes! That's what my ex-husband calls him. But his name is Gale, after my father, Gale White."

Holly needed no further proof that she'd connected with Snake's mother. "Your boy is safe with me," she assured the woman.

"Thank God!" She started sobbing.

"There's no need to cry anymore. Everything is going to be fine, Mrs. Ferrell," Holly said soothingly. She blinked away her own tears. She would never get *her* boy back.

Chapter Eight

Mrs. Ferrell flew in from Philadelphia that afternoon, and Philip and Holly took Snake to the airport to meet her. The moment Snake spotted his mother across the terminal he let go of Holly's hand and ran to her. And she ran to him, arms wide in welcome.

"Like one of those slow-motion TV commercials," Philip commented, observing the mother-and-child reunion with a wide grin. He glanced at Holly, and his happy expression turned to one of concern. "Are you all right? You look like you're about to faint."

"Nonsense. I'm fine." But she leaned against his solid frame as she watched the woman and boy hug and kiss.

After a moment Snake pointed to Holly and Philip, and Mrs. Ferrell rushed to them.

"How can I ever thank you enough?" she asked.

Holly guessed Mrs. Ferrell's age to be close to her own. Snake had inherited her brown eyes, narrow face and delicate bone structure.

"Holly was the one who insisted we try to find you," Philip told her. "She sensed something was amiss with Snake's situation."

"From the little Gale told me about you," Holly said, preferring to use the boy's real name, "I knew you couldn't have walked out on him without a word, Mrs. Ferrell."

"Please. Call me Susan," the mother said, offering Holly her hand. "I thought he understood that I would be gone for only two weeks. But my ex-husband must have convinced him otherwise."

"You never even phoned once," Snake said, but when he turned his eyes up to her, there was total forgiveness and love in his look.

"Sweetie, I explained that I would be on a sailboat. I *did* call you when we docked the following week, but by that time your father had taken off with you."

"At first I didn't believe Dad when he said you weren't coming back. Then I gave up hoping."

"My poor baby." She hugged the boy close to her side. "How horrible these last three weeks must have been for you."

"I'm not a baby," he corrected. "And it wasn't so bad. Dad let me do anything I wanted. *He* didn't treat me like a baby. But now he's in big trouble because he hit a car and didn't stop. I told him he should, but he said he couldn't chance dealing with the cops. So we just kept going."

"Oh, Lord. I didn't realize that you were in the car with him. You could have been killed!"

"Nah, it was just a sideswipe. No one was hurt. Are you gonna help him out, Mom?"

Susan shook her head slowly but emphatically. "I'm through helping your father out of his jams, Gale." She turned to Holly and Philip. "Joe's always been irresponsible, but I never dreamed he was capable of kidnapping his own son to get back at me for remarrying."

"That seems a pretty drastic measure to ruin an ex-wife's honeymoon," Philip remarked.

"Oh, he didn't do it just for spite. Joe truly loves Gale and felt their relationship was threatened when I remarried. So he acted on his first impulse. I want to believe he would have eventually come to his senses and brought Gale back himself."

"Dad said we were going to travel all around the world together," Snake informed her.

"Sure." Susan gave her son a sad smile. "And the moon and back, too, I suppose. Your father is more a child than you are, Gale. You'll understand that some day, I hope."

"Are we gonna go see him now?"

"No. We're returning to Philadelphia on the next flight, sweetie. We have a new place to live now. A lovely house in the suburbs."

"I'll hate it there," Snake assured her.

"You'll love it," she insisted. "Now say goodbye to these two wonderful people."

The boy hugged Holly and Philip. Then Susan hugged them. Then everybody hugged one another all over again.

But when Snake turned away, he didn't look back. "Mom," they heard him say as he walked toward the boarding gate hand in hand with her. "Will I be going to a new school?"

"Yes, and you're going to have a lot of work to make up. But I'll help you."

"Listen, Mom, I don't want the kids at this new school to know my real name is Gale. That's a girl's name."

"It's a lovely name. Much nicer than Snake. Where'd you get that awful leather jacket?"

"Dad bought it for me. Mom, don't be mad at him. I know what he did wasn't right but..." The sound of his voice drifted away.

"There goes our *baku*," Philip said. "It seems we were stuck with him for a lifetime, but it's been less than twenty-four hours. I have to admit I was getting pretty attached to him, though."

Holly said nothing. It was as if she were in a trance, staring after the boy long after he'd disappeared from view.

"You were great with him, Holly," Philip continued. "You have a special way with kids. Snake really warmed up to you."

"He's already forgotten all about me," she said brusquely, shoving her hand into her pocket. Her fingers wrapped around the Goddess of Joy. "I was just a temporary substitute mother for him."

Philip put his arm around her. "Ever think about being a real one some day?"

"No. Not anymore." She shrugged off his arm and headed out of the terminal.

"Holly, wait! Did I say something wrong?"

She stopped and turned to him. "Oh, Philip. Hold me. Please hold me for a minute."

He took her into the warm cocoon of his big, strong arms and rocked her side to side in his embrace. They were oblivious to the people streaming past them. "I want to hold you forever, sweetheart," Philip whispered. "I'm falling in love with you."

His words were balm to her soul but also pricked her conscience. "You don't know anything about me," she said, leaning her face against the wall of his chest.

She could feel the vibration as he laughed softly. "Do you have some terrible secret in your past, Holly?"

She pushed away to look up at his face. "It's time I told you about my past, Philip. But not here."

"No, not here. I'll take you home." He took her arm and guided her out of the busy terminal.

She'd assumed Philip had meant her apartment, but when he told his driver to take them to Fairfield, she hadn't objected. They'd spoken little during the ride, and now, sipping a glass of wine with Philip in his tower, Holly had no inclination to talk at all. She felt totally drained after fighting so many emotions all day. She closed her eyes and imagined Snake and his mother sitting close together on the plane, making plans for the future.

King Kong had welcomed Holly with his usual exuberance, then settled beside her on the sofa and placed his shaggy head in her lap. As she abstractedly scratched him behind the ears, the big dog wheezed with pleasure. Philip sat across from them on a creaky rocking chair. Holly found comfort in the peaceful sounds from the dog and the chair. She opened her eyes and reached for her wineglass on the low wooden table in front of her. She took a small sip.

"Now that we're alone, I'm finding it difficult to open up to you, Philip," she admitted.

"I find talking about myself difficult, too," he said. "But we don't have to talk at all. I'm perfectly content to just sit here and look at you, Holly. The sun is sending its last rays of light through the window behind you, and there's a bright golden halo around your hair." He grinned. "Madonna and dog."

Holly took a deeper sip of wine. "I once had a dog named Lucky," she said. "A big, lovable mutt like yours. I was really fond of that dog."

"What happened to him?"

"Oh, I gave him to my brother in Vermont."

Philip rocked a few times. "Why'd you give him away if you were so fond of him?"

"For his own good." Holly turned her head, splitting the halo of sunlight with her profile. "Lucky missed having a child around to play with, and my brother has three."

Philip stopped rocking. "What child did Lucky miss so much, Holly?"

"Mine." She drank again and put down her glass. "Danny. He was named after his father and took after him, too. Not only in appearance. They were both so cheerful and easygoing." She smiled softly, sadly. "And they were both crazy about fishing. They'd even go fishing in the winter."

Holly's revelation that she'd had a child stunned Philip. He waited for her to continue, but only silence followed. He didn't break it, sensing that she could only tell him what had happened in her own good time, in her own convoluted way. The only sound now was his dog's deep sighs as Holly continued to scratch him behind the ear.

"Ever been ice fishing, Philip?" she asked after a moment.

He shook his head. He assumed her non sequitur was somehow relevant and hoped that if he said as little as possible, she would keep talking.

"What you do is cut holes in the ice, then wait for the fish to take the bait on the end of the tip-up lines," she explained in an expressionless voice. "I went out a few times with Daniel and Danny, but I usually got too cold standing around waiting for the fish to bite. Danny never minded the cold, though. He was a rugged little kid. So he and his dad went out to the lake every Saturday during the winter while I stayed home with a good book. They'd bring home pickerel. Not my favorite fish. Too bony. I used to worry about Danny choking on the bones, but he never did. You worry about so many things that never happen. And the things you never worry about *do*."

"Let me turn on some lights," Philip said, getting up from his chair.

Holly hadn't even noticed that the sun had set and the room had become shadowy. Philip flicked on a lamp, slipped off his suit jacket and tie, then sat beside her on the sofa. He took her free hand as she continued to stroke King with the other. The dog snored blissfully. Holly rested her head against Philip's shoulder.

"I like it here in your tower," she said. "I feel as if the rest of the world doesn't exist. That there's only the two of us."

"And King," Philip added. And her ghosts from the past, he thought.

"You know, I haven't talked this much in years," she told him. "I used to be a real chatterbox. I used to be a lot of things I'm not anymore."

Philip gently kneaded her slender fingers with his. "Tell me more, Holly."

"About ice fishing?"

"Whatever you want to talk about, sweetheart."

Holly took a deep breath. She'd talked circles and circles around what she needed to tell him, and the circles were getting smaller as she came closer to it. She adjusted her head against his shoulder. If she moved her cheek just right, it fit perfectly into a special, comfortable place just below his collarbone.

"You're a very patient listener," she told him.

"Not really," he refuted. "In fact, I tend to be too impatient with most people. But I'll listen to you all night, Holly. You fascinate me. You have from the moment we met."

"You were very impatient with *me* when we met," she reminded him.

"And you weren't?" he countered. "How you glared at me when I walked into your classroom! The flash from your eyes was like blue lightning. What did you think I was, some Martian invader?"

"Don't be silly. I'm smart enough to know that Martian invaders wear shiny silver space suits, not faded jeans."

"Then why did you look at me with such horror? Surely you can't find faded jeans that offensive."

"I thought you were bringing me bad news. I always assume strangers bring bad news."

"Why?"

The image of the policeman standing at her door flashed in her mind. She pulled away from Philip and stood up. He watched as she paced around the room, her eyes looking at everything but seeing nothing.

"I used to worry about Danny getting chilled when he went ice fishing," she said. "So I bought him a pair of skates for Christmas, and a pair for his father, too. Go skating with Danny while you're out on the lake, I told Daniel. It'll keep you both warm. Wasn't that a good idea?"

"Come and sit beside me, Holly," Philip said.

"Wasn't that a good idea?" she asked again, keeping her distance.

"Yes," he replied. But he'd already guessed the end to her story.

She nodded and continued. "Daniel thought it was a good idea, too. The next time he took Danny out to the lake, they brought their skates along. The ice was at least six inches thick. Perfectly safe. The other fishermen who were there that day assured me of that.

Nobody had the slightest reason to be concerned as Daniel skated away, pulling Danny behind him."

Holly stopped talking again and intently studied the paperback titles on Philip's bookshelf. She drew one out and leafed through it. "I've never been a big Hemingway fan myself," she commented in a shaky voice.

"Holly, please." Philip rose and slowly walked to her. He took the book from her and placed it on the shelf. "Tell me what happened."

"It was a fluke of nature, really," she replied, her voice controlled and steady now. "A little natural spring under the ice, making one patch much thinner than the rest. It cracked, and they both disappeared. Some men ran to help them. Others ran to call an ambulance. But nobody could save them. They went under fast with their heavy clothes and skates, and they were lost."

Philip gathered her into his arms. "I'm so sorry," he whispered into her hair.

"It happened a long time ago, Philip," she replied wearily. "Four years ago last January. I've done my best to get on with my life, and I'm managing to do that much better lately. But I'm not the same person I was before it happened, and I never will be again. That innate joy that was once part of me died with them."

"It could be resurrected again," he said softly.

"No." She lifted her chin to look at him. "That's why I told you this, Philip. I want you to understand that I'm no longer capable of a limitless love. All I can offer you is a deep, abiding affection. I can't risk giving more."

Optimist that he was, he refused to believe her and kissed her with a lingering gentleness.

Holly didn't want his gentleness now, though. Or his sympathy. She wanted sheer, physical release. She wanted to lose herself in him. Her physical desire for Philip no longer shocked or frightened her. She accepted it as natural and inevitable. The past would always be with her. She had no choice but to accept that, Holly realized. But she also realized that she was ready to start living her life in the present again.

She broke away from Philip's arms. "Do you want to make love with me?" she asked him bluntly. She was being more blunt than she had ever been with a man before, even her husband.

"Oh, Holly." He let out a shuddering breath. "That's like asking me if I want the sun to rise tomorrow. But I don't want to rush you."

She could not want a finer man, she decided. For all his proclaimed impatience, he was being so patient with her. She reached up and touched his taut face, feeling the heat of his skin against her fingertips. Only one thing was stopping her now. And she told him. "There's nothing I want more than to be with you now, Philip. But I'm not protected."

"I'll take care of that," he promised her.

"Then there's nothing stopping us, is there?"

She led the way to the circular staircase and began the tricky climb up the narrow iron steps. She almost lost her nerve but continued up, not daring to look down. Or back. She had warned Philip of her limitations; she had explained why they existed. And if he chose to follow her, that meant he'd accepted them.

She felt his hand at the small of her back and smiled. He'd accepted.

When they reached his bedroom, she almost lost her nerve again, though. Moonlight flooding through the long arched windows bathed the room in a luminous glow. As beautiful as it was, Holly wished there were shades that could be drawn. In her sudden shyness, she longed for darkness. She turned to Philip with a brave smile and began unbuttoning the front of her high-necked dress with trembling fingers.

"I haven't made love in a very long time," she informed him in a small, timid voice. "Not since I lost my hus—"

"Stop!" Philip commanded, clutching her fumbling hands. Then he softened his voice. "Let me undress you." He brought her hands to his lips and kissed each of her fingers, not missing one. "Slowly. Very slowly."

What Holly really wanted to do was strip as quickly as possible then scurry under the covers. She was no longer the brazen girl parading on the wharf in her first bikini. She was a mature, self-conscious woman who was apprehensive about unveiling her body to a man for the first time.

But Philip soon made her overcome her inhibitions. He carefully undressed her, taking his time, murmuring his appreciation as he did so. If undressing a woman could be considered an art, he certainly was a master of it. There was no fumbling, no awkwardness. He kissed each inch of flesh he bared until Holly tingled all over, then he stroked and fondled her, turning the tingle into a shimmering heat.

"You take my breath away, Holly," he told her when she stood before him naked, her small rounded breasts high and proud. "You're so beautiful."

And she believed him, or at least believed that to *him* she was. The way he gazed at her made her feel more beautiful and desirable than she'd thought possible.

She took a deep breath. "My turn," she said and began unbuttoning his shirt. His chest was as she'd imagined it—brawny, muscular, rock-hard. She trailed her lips from his collarbone to his rib cage, lightly brushing across the dark mat of hair. The vital, springy texture of it thrilled her.

He chuckled softly. "That tickles."

"Oh, so you're ticklish, are you?"

"Extremely."

"I'll keep that in mind," she said, unbuckling his belt. As she inched down his zipper he groaned.

"Sweetheart, you don't have to take as much time undressing me," he said. "I don't think I can stand it."

"Then sit down," she advised, pushing him down on the bed.

She slipped off his shoes, peeled off his socks and tickled his feet.

"Stop!" he begged, laughing, and as the sound of it boomed through the moonlit room, she pulled down his trousers.

Yes, he was just as strapping and fit and powerful as she'd imagined. She almost lost her nerve again, though, as her fingers slipped under the elastic band of his briefs. Since when had she become so brazen?

"I take it back. *Don't* stop," Philip urged.

Never one to leave what she'd started unfinished, she tugged down his briefs. With a sharp intake of breath she looked away, then back again. His virility was even more than she'd imagined.

Philip grinned at her wide-eyed expression. "You're an absolute delight, Holly Murphey," he said, grabbing her by her slender waist and pulling her down beside him.

Delight. That's what they gave each other as they kissed and nuzzled. Their caresses were both playful and erotic, demanding yet gentle. Holly pulsed with want for Philip as he explored her body, testing it, tasting it, finding her pleasure points with his clever hands and tongue.

Philip took his sweet time with her. He wanted this first time together to last for as long as possible. He wanted Holly to trust him completely, then give herself completely. He refused, absolutely, to believe that she was incapable of ever feeling love and joy again. He would prove her wrong. Maybe not now, not tonight, but eventually. As he stroked the exquisite silkiness of her inner thighs, she moaned. The moan came from deep within her throat, and he loved the sound of it. Her face was flushed, her breasts swollen, her nipples budded with arousal from his caresses. He lowered his mouth and sucked them again, and she gasped with pleasure. He raised his face to stare at her, to take in her abandonment.

Holly saw herself in Philip's heated gaze—her nakedness, her shameless pleasure, her avid need to please and be pleased. She gloried in his recognition of her voluptuousness. She had no secrets from him. She wanted him to know how sensual, how reckless she felt with him. But there existed deep within her a fear that surfaced above her recklessness—her fear of becoming pregnant.

"Don't forget. I'm not protected," she whispered.

"Of course I won't, sweetheart," he assured her.

It halted their lovemaking for only a moment, and then, unable to hold back any longer, he eased her thighs apart and slowly entered her. She yielded, soft and ready and quivering, and wrapped her legs around his broad torso. He delved deeper and deeper into her silken chamber until he reached the very quick of her.

Holly called out his name, over and over again, as Philip moved with her in perfect unison. And then, at last, the sweet release flooded through her. He continued to move in time with her thundering heartbeat until he, too, found release and shuddered with pleasure.

"My wonderful, wonderful woman," he whispered.

A short while later Philip awoke to the sweet scent and feel of Holly nestled against him and to the sound of King's barking downstairs. It was lucky the dog feared climbing the open flight of steps leading to the bedroom, Philip thought, or he would have bounded into the bed with them by now—or at a more inopportune moment.

Philip waited a moment, reluctant to leave Holly, but the barking continued. Taking care not to disturb Holly, he got up. She tossed and turned for a moment but didn't awake. When she rolled onto her stomach, Philip smiled. So *that* was her favorite sleeping position.

He went to get a blanket out of the chest across the room. On the way he gathered up Holly's pale underthings and dark dress, still smiling as he recalled the pleasure of helping her out of them. He placed the garments on a chair and took the blanket to the bed.

But he couldn't bring himself to cover Holly with it right away. The sight of her naked body, bathed in moonlight, made him ache with desire all over again. And with love. Her smooth, silky skin shimmered like polished ivory yet pulsed with warmth, with life. She was far more lovely to him than any inanimate goddess could ever be. He regarded her for a long moment, then King's continued racket brought him out of his reverie. With a sigh of regret, he placed the blanket over her and quickly dressed and went downstairs.

King was in the kitchen area, barking at his bowl on the counter. Philip filled it for him, then sat at the table to keep him company. Unlike most animals, King appreciated a little conversation while he ate. Or at least Philip was convinced that he did. When he'd told Holly that he and his dog had deep philosophical discussions when they were alone, he'd only been half joking. Philip had grown into the habit of talking things out with King.

"She's the one I've been waiting for," he announced to his canine companion.

King looked up from his bowl.

"That's right, pal. It's serious. I'd ask Holly to move in with me if I thought she'd accept. But first I have to convince her that we can be happy together. And that's going to take some doing. Holly's lost so much, she can't seem to believe in lasting happiness. But maybe I have enough belief for both of us."

King resumed eating.

"I've been searching all these years since my divorce for a woman I could connect with completely," Philip continued. "I'd almost given up finding her. And then the Goddess of Joy led me to Holly. It's easy to imagine spending the rest of my life with her. But I don't know..."

His voice trailed off. King nosed his empty bowl across the floor, then gave his full attention to Philip by coming over to him and placing his head on his knee. He gazed up at his master with soulful eyes.

"It may not work out," Philip told him. "Holly's put up protective walls around her heart, and I don't know if I can break through them. The only thing I know for sure is that she's everything I want in a woman. She's mature, intelligent and sensitive. She has all the qualities my ex-wife lacked. Hey, she even likes mutts like you." He patted King's head. "And to top it off, she's beautiful. I don't mean that flashy, look-at-me kind of beauty. Hers goes much deeper and lasts a lot longer. When Holly's eighty, she'll still be beautiful. And I'll tell you another thing about her, King." Philip lowered his voice. "Now this is strictly between you and me. She's the most satisfying woman I've ever made love with."

Stating this aloud, Philip felt a sharp, hot need for her in his loins. "So what the hell am I wasting time talking to you for, pal, when *she's* upstairs in my bed?" He stood abruptly. "Go take a nap, King. I'm going to wake Holly up from hers."

The phone rang, and Philip glared at it. He decided not to pick it up, and listened to the message the caller left instead. It turned out to be one of the more influential members of his board of directors, demanding that Philip explain why he'd canceled the meeting today.

Philip hissed a short expletive. He didn't like explaining himself to anyone. But as the head of a growing corporation he felt obliged to do just that to board members and investors. Every risk he took affected so many people, including the employees who relied on Irons Building and Development, Incorporated for their livelihoods. At times Philip longed for the days when he'd been flat broke but fancy-free, a carpenter by trade and a dreamer by inclination. That time was long past, though, he reminded himself.

But he still had his dreams, Philip thought as he began to mount the stairs to his bedroom. The project he was trying to push through now was one he'd dreamed about for a long time. Nobody believed in it the way he did, though. He'd made a tactical error when he'd canceled the board meeting. He'd known it at the time but did it anyway. He may have been chief executive officer of a corporation, but he was still a free agent, wasn't he? And as a free agent, a free *soul*, he'd decided it was more important to help Holly find a little boy's mother. He didn't regret his decision one bit.

Holly was waiting for him at the top of the stairs, fully dressed.

"I want to go home now," she told him.

Chapter Nine

"I was hoping you'd spend the night with me, sweetheart."

Holly avoided Philip's eyes. "I don't think that's a good idea."

"I think it's a terrific idea," Philip insisted. His face took on a determined set. He wasn't going to let her pull away from him.

"I wouldn't feel comfortable spending the night here," she told him. In truth, she feared that the longer she stayed, the more difficult it would be to leave. That was the danger in loving someone. You became dependent on that love, and when it was taken away, you almost died, too. Never again, Holly had promised herself. She could never risk experiencing such pain again. "I think it's best that you take me home now."

Philip refused to be put off by her aloof demeanor. "What's the rush? At least stay and have dinner with me first." He put his arms around her waist and began massaging the small of her back.

It felt marvelous, both soothing and sensual, and Holly's firm resolution to leave as soon as possible softened. She didn't have the heart to refuse his simple request. "All right," she said. "I'll stay for dinner. But then I want to go home."

He smiled. "We'll see."

"I mean it, Philip."

His smile never wavered. Taking her hand, he led her down to the kitchen area.

"I haven't gotten around to shopping for groceries lately," he admitted, opening the refrigerator door.

"Obviously," Holly said, peering over his shoulder and taking in the meager contents of the refrigerator—five tall brown bottles of beer, a rusty head of lettuce, a wedge of cheese, three eggs and a covered ironstone baking dish. "We could share a cheese omelet," she suggested.

"Why not warm up the lasagna we had the last time you were here?" Philip said, pointing to the baking dish.

Holly laughed. "I doubt it's still edible."

"Sure it is. It's only been in the fridge for a few days. Four at the most."

Four at the most! Holly's mind jolted with the realization that she'd known Philip for less than a week. She'd known Daniel for more than ten years before they'd become physically intimate. And their first union had still been uncomfortable and awkward.

Of course she'd been young and inexperienced then, and so had Daniel. Now she was a mature woman, and Philip had proved to be an expert lover. Yet it didn't seem quite right to her that she had found such sublime satisfaction in a man's embrace after knowing him for less than a week.

This was all happening too fast for her, Holly decided. She needed time alone to think. "I'm really not very hungry, Philip," she said. "I'd just like to go home now."

He slammed the refrigerator door shut. "You're having regrets about making love with me, aren't you?"

Holly saw the hurt in his eyes, and her heart melted. She lifted her hand and caressed his cheek. "No regrets," she assured him. "What we shared was wonderful. Glorious. But I'm afraid of getting too involved with you. I've been alone for a long time. Please try to understand."

Philip took a deep breath. "I do understand. But that doesn't make it any easier for me to let you go now. I want you so much, sweetheart. I want you to stay."

The longing in his voice captured her even before his mouth covered hers. Still, she kept her lips shut and unyielding for a good five seconds at least. Then she gave in to his persuasive power over her and opened her mouth to his, wrapping her arms around his waist to pull him closer. She wanted, needed the pressure of his big body against hers again. When she felt his desire against her abdomen, she was inordinately pleased that she had such power over him, too. His kiss became more demanding, and she answered his demand with equal force.

Philip tore his lips from hers and picked her up. She felt as light as a cloud in his arms. "I think we're both hungry for something more than dinner," he said.

Holly supported his statement by nibbling at his ear as he carried her upstairs. She guessed she'd be spending the night after all.

"The usual, honey?" Gladys asked when Holly took her regular seat at the counter of Dino's Diner the next morning.

"No, I'll have pancakes for a change," Holly replied.

"You kidding?" Gladys looked at her as if she'd requested something shocking.

Holly laughed. "With bacon, please. I've got quite an appetite this morning."

"Well, I'm glad you're feeling better," the waitress said.

"Better? I haven't been ill."

"Oh." Gladys shrugged. "When you didn't show up here yesterday, Pops and I figured you must have been sick."

Holly hadn't even considered that Mr. Brakenbiddle would be concerned. "No, I'm fine. Just fine," she assured Gladys.

As Holly waited for her breakfast, a dreamy little smile lifted her lips. She'd parted with Philip in front of her apartment house an hour ago, but in her mind she was still with him. He'd driven her to New Haven himself—in a shiny green pickup truck! He'd explained it was his vehicle of choice when he wasn't being driven around in his limousine. Holly's smile broadened as she recalled his words. "You can take the boy out of the truck, but you can't take the truck out of the boy."

What a study in contrasts Philip was, she mused. She really knew so little about him. At the same time she felt she knew his very soul. But that was ridiculous. She didn't even know such basic facts as his birthday, his weight, his middle name, his favorite color. Red! she decided. It suited his dynamic personality. Besides, the quilt covering his bed was red.

Her thoughts strayed to their night in that bed. She wondered if they would ever run out of ways to delight each other. She doubted it. She couldn't wait until she was with him again.

Tonight! She'd invited him to her place for dinner. She wanted it to be special. Veal cordon bleu—the fanciest dish she knew how to prepare. She'd go grocery shopping right after classes. And she'd buy a bottle of wine and some candles and a bouquet of flowers for the table. And while she was at it, a tablecloth and wineglasses, too. She hadn't entertained since moving to New Haven. She'd also buy new sheets for her bed—romantic and frilly ones. And a sexy, flattering nightgown. She laughed at herself. She certainly lacked the basic accoutrements for conducting a mad, passionate affair.

"May I join you, Mrs. Murphey?" a familiar voice asked, interrupting her thoughts.

"Mr. Brakenbiddle! Please do."

"You don't know how relieved I am to see you here today, my dear," the elderly antique dealer told her. "I called you last night to see how you were feeling and became alarmed when you didn't answer the phone."

"I'm sorry you worried about me," Holly said sincerely. At the same time she felt a stab of impatience. Surely she wasn't obliged to check in with Mr. Brakenbiddle every time she broke her normal routine. Guilt immediately replaced the impatience. Since she'd never broken her routine in all the years he'd known her, naturally he would worry.

"If you didn't show up here again today, I was going to go to the academy to find out what had happened to you," he informed her.

"I'm sorry," she said again, placing her hand on his arm. "It never occurred to me that you would be so concerned, but it should have. I would have been just as concerned about you."

"Ah, well." He patted her hand. "You're back again, and that's all that counts. Another lovely day, isn't it?"

Relieved that he hadn't asked her to explain her absence, Holly gave him an appreciative smile. "It couldn't be lovelier," she agreed enthusiastically.

Gladys placed a plate of pancakes and bacon in front of her.

"Lady Gladys, what's come over you?" Mr. Brakenbiddle asked. "That's not Holly's order."

"It is today, Pops. Are you going to switch on me, too?"

"Heavens, no. My tea and muffin, please."

"Coming up."

Mr. Brakenbiddle shook his head in wonderment as he watched Holly spread butter over her pancakes. "I can't believe my eyes," he said.

She rolled hers. "I can just see tonight's headline in the *New Haven Register*. Holly Murphey Changed Her Breakfast Order! Quite an earthshaking event. Would you like a slice of bacon?"

Mr. Brakenbiddle turned up his nose and sniffed. "All fat and salt," he said curtly.

He was out of sorts, Holly knew, because she hadn't volunteered any information about her whereabouts the day before. And she wasn't going to, either. She didn't want to tell Mr. Brakenbiddle that she'd become involved with Philip Irons. She didn't want to tell anybody until she understood her feelings better. Right now she was in a state of excitement and confusion. Her quiet, circumspect life had been turned upside down, inside out.

She mollified the antique dealer by asking him about his latest sales and acquisitions, and soon they were chatting away as usual. They walked arm and arm down the street after breakfast and parted at the corner, friends again.

Holly had scheduled an essay exam for her last class. She wrote the questions on the board, passed out composition notebooks, then settled down at her desk to write a list of things to do in preparation for Philip's visit. It was such a long list! She realized she'd been foolish to invite Philip to dinner that evening.

But as they'd shared a farewell kiss in front of her apartment house, it had seemed like such a good idea. She'd had an overwhelming urge to cook for him.

She reconsidered the menu. Perhaps the veal was too ambitious. Perhaps the whole idea was too ambitious. She should have gone along with Philip's original suggestion of having dinner at a restaurant. Better yet, she should have told him she couldn't see him this evening. She didn't want him to become a habit, after all.

Yet she *wanted* to see him. All day she'd been longing for him. She missed his grin, his touch, his soft, low voice. She missed the scent of him, the sight of him, the warmth and excitement his presence brought her. That he'd become so ingrained in her mind, her heart, her senses after such a short time bothered her. It bothered her so much that she wished they weren't getting together for a while. Yet she *wanted* to see him. No matter how she vacillated, that remained constant.

She looked at the wall clock. "You have twenty-five minutes remaining to complete the exam," she announced to her students. "Please note that the last question requires an example from both *Hamlet* and *King Lear*. And remember that spelling counts."

Her remarks produced a spate of groaning and muttering, but the girls soon settled down to work again, and Holly left the classroom for a drink of water. She discovered Philip lounging in the hall, and her heart jumped into high gear and started hammering.

"Aw, Mrs. Murphey, does spelling *really* count?" he asked.

She had to stop herself from rushing into his arms. She glanced up and down the hall, relieved that it was empty. His last visit had produced enough speculation. A second one would start it up all over again.

"What are you doing here," she asked a bit breathlessly. The unexpected sight of him always took her breath away.

"I had to see you before I left for Sweden."

She laughed, assuming that he was joking. "You'll be back in time for dinner, won't you?"

"I wish! I'm afraid we're not going to be having dinner together for at least a week. Unless you want to come to Sweden with me. Do you have a passport?"

She shook her head. She could almost believe that he was serious now. The idea of flying around the world with Philip caught her fancy, but only for a moment. "This isn't just an elaborate excuse to get out of our date tonight, is it?"

"Oh, sweetheart, that's the last thing I want to do. But I'm needed as a consultant for a condominium project in Göteborg. The architect called me. They're having construction problems. It's an opportunity I can't pass up because it's exactly the kind of project I want to do here. Besides, I feel damn flattered that my expertise is so valued." He grinned. "Hell, I never even heard of Göteborg until today!"

Holly grinned back, pleased for him, proud of him. "Obviously they'd heard of *you*, though. I didn't realize you had an international reputation as a builder, Philip."

"I don't," he replied, waving away such a claim to fame. "I just happened to have worked on some successful projects with the architect in the past.'' His grin dissolved as his eyes grew serious. ''Are you going to miss me, Holly?''

She nodded. ''I've been missing you since this morning,'' she admitted.

''Same here. I'm glad you spent the night with me. Those memories are going to have to last me for the week.''

His fingertips touched her cheek; his soft voice touched her heart. Holly attempted a smile. ''I'm sure those memories will pale the moment you get off the plane and meet your first tall, blond Viking princess.''

''A Viking princess.'' Philip's laugh was scoffing. ''I've got much better than that right here.'' His fingers glided over Holly's cheekbone and trailed into her short, dark hair. ''I have a real goddess.''

''I'm hardly that,'' Holly said.

''You are to me,'' Philip told her.

Footsteps! Holly moved away from Philip so quickly she almost lost her balance. She turned to see a chubby girl stomping down the hall toward them. It was Shirley Podemicki, the self-styled sleuth.

''How you doing, Mrs. Murphey?'' the girl asked cheerily, her smile broad and knowing as she glanced at Philip.

Holly put her finger to her lips. ''My class is in the middle of an exam. Let's not disturb their concentration, Shirley.''

''Or yours, Mrs. Murphey?'' she asked in a lower voice filled with insinuation.

Holly pulled back her shoulders and put her hands on her hips. "Why are you roaming the halls, Shirley? Shouldn't you be in class?" She held her breath, expecting the girl to put the same question to her.

But if Shirley thought to ask it, she let it slide by, more interested in giving Philip a once-over. "Are you the guy Melissa told us about?" she asked him. "The one in the black sweatshirt?"

"I've been known to wear one," he admitted, keeping a straight face.

"And did you send a big box of pastries to Mrs. Murphey the other day?"

"I recall doing something like that."

"Then you're Mr. Irons," the girl deduced. She gave Philip one last, long look, smiled her approval then continued clumping down the hall.

Philip moved close to Holly again. "Can we go some place a little more private for a moment?"

She considered the possibilities. There were always a few teachers in the faculty lounge. The courtyard was visible from almost every classroom window. All the administrative offices were occupied. She sighed. "I'm afraid not."

"Then I'll have to chance kissing you goodbye right here."

"Wait, I just thought of a place." Holly took his hand and led him to the supply room. It smelled of pencils and paper, glue and cardboard. A small, gritty window, sealed forever with layers of paint, let in dull, opaque light. She closed the door behind them and giggled like a schoolgirl.

"I must be crazy," she said. She stood on tiptoe, wrapped her arms around his neck and pressed her lips to his.

How she adored kissing him. It felt so right, so perfect. She fought down the temptation to cling to him, to beg him to stay. She knew she was being foolish about it. Hadn't she just been wishing for some time away from him to sort out her emotions? But if only they could have one more night together before he left.

"Can't you leave tomorrow?" she asked him.

"No, they want me there as soon as possible," he said with regret in his voice. "I'm flying out of New York this evening. But I had to say goodbye to you in person first."

They kissed again, softly, sweetly. "Will you call me the moment you get back?" she asked.

"You know I will. And I'll think about you every moment I'm away." He drank her in with a long, lingering gaze, then reclaimed her lips with more urgency. He cupped her breasts through the thin material of her blouse, coaxing the nipples with his thumbs until they hardened. She opened her mouth to him with a sigh, and his tongue delved into the moist velvet of it. How he wanted her, needed her right here and now, in this dingy little supply room crowded with boxes and rickety shelves.

"No! We can't," she gasped as if reading his mind. She leaned back in his arms, her face flushed. "Have we gone completely out of our minds, Philip? We're getting carried away like two adolescents with raging hormones."

"Yeah, isn't it wonderful?" He lowered his head to take her mouth again.

But she pushed him away, laughing. It *was* wonderful to have this rush of excitement whenever he touched her. But it was absurd, too. And scary. It made her feel so out of control. She was a responsible teacher, an example to her students, not some dizzy little nitwit in the throes of her first hot love affair.

They heard a crash in the back of the room, and Holly's eyes widened in horror. Philip released her and went to investigate. "It's nothing," he said. "Just a box that fell from a shelf."

"The ghost of Isabel Jerome must have pushed it," Holly said dryly. "Oh, Philip, I hate to say this, but you'd better leave. I have to get back to my class."

"Just one more kiss and I will."

"Better not to risk it."

He took it anyway, a quick, hard one. Then a peck on her nose for good measure. "Take care, love." He opened the door slowly and peeked out. "Coast is clear. I'll make a run for it," he dramatically declared. Then he was gone.

Holly waited in the storeroom until her flush and excitement subsided. When she returned to her classroom, no one even glanced up. Her absence, thank goodness, hadn't been noticed. She thought of a Mae West line and smiled to herself. *Goodness had nothing to do with it, dearie.*

When Celia called and asked her to go shopping on Saturday morning, Holly accepted, although she loathed shopping, especially for clothes. But her wardrobe could do with a little perking up, she'd decided. Besides, she didn't want to nip Celia's friendly overtures in the bud.

They met at Macy's, and Celia immediately began selecting clothes for Holly to try on. "You've got to start putting a little color in your life," she said.

"I have," Holly assured her. She took the orange and purple dress Celia was pushing at her and put it back on the rack. She selected a light gray one with a rounded white collar instead, much more her style. She'd never gone in for bright colors, even as a teenager. She did find a red cotton sweater that appealed to her, though, and bought that, too. Celia approved.

They went to the Chapel Square Mall next, and Holly's eyes began to glaze over as Celia dragged her from one store to another. She would have been happy to have called it quits after Macy's, but Celia's philosophy was to Shop 'til You Drop.

Holly's attention perked up, though, when they went into a charming little lingerie boutique. She couldn't resist an ivory satin and lace bra, matching panties and garter belt, gossamer sheer hose, a wispy white gown with a halter neckline dipping into a stretch-lace bodice and a silk robe the color of a blush. Celia's eyebrows almost shot up to her hairline when Holly made these purchases.

"Let's break for lunch and have a little heart-to-heart talk, Hol," she said.

If she hadn't suggested it, Holly would have. She desperately needed to confide in someone about the turmoil in her heart. Someone who would understand.

They went to Fitzwilly's and both ordered a glass of white wine and a slice of asparagus quiche.

"So level with me, Hol." Celia sampled her wine. "Is there a man in your life?"

"Yes," Holly replied, eyes glowing. "His name is Philip Irons, and he's wonderful. He makes *me* feel wonderful. He's been away on a business trip these last few days, and I can't stop thinking about him." She pushed her wineglass around on the table. "I had hoped I could have an affair with him and still keep my emotions under control." Her voice cracked. "But it's so difficult not to love him."

Celia gave her an encouraging smile. "So why shouldn't you love him, honey?" Her expression changed from approval to censure. "Oh, I get it. He's married."

"No! Of course not! You know me better than that, Ce."

"I didn't mean that you'd intentionally get involved with a married man, Hol." She stabbed at her quiche. "But it can happen to the best of us. Take me, for example."

"You?" Holly frowned. "Frank?"

"That's right. Mr. Nice Guy turned out to be Mr. Sleaze. A wife and three kiddies in Wallingford. One of his softball buddies clued me in."

"I'm sorry, Celia."

"Yeah, that makes two of us." She shrugged. "Luckily I found out in time, though. Before I got too involved. But tell me more about this Philip. If he's not married, what's the problem?"

"I'm afraid he cares for me more than he should," Holly replied softly.

"I don't get it."

"I'm not the right woman for him, Ce." Holly took a deep breath. "I know we'll have to end our affair eventually. But I just want a little time, a little happiness with him before that time comes. Is that terribly selfish?"

"Selfish?" Celia looked puzzled. "Take all the happiness you can get, Hol. Lord knows you deserve it."

"But it isn't fair to Philip! He needs a woman who'll share his life." She paused for a heartbeat. "Who'll have children with him."

"Why shouldn't that woman be you?" Celia pressed. "Everyone in the family prays that you'll have a second chance at marriage and children, Holly."

And their prayers were in vain, Holly thought. She would never take that chance again. How could she dare plan a future with someone, knowing how easily it could be destroyed?

"When I lost Daniel and Danny, I lost all my hopes and dreams, too," she told her sister-in-law. She saw the tears spring to Celia's eyes and blinked away her own. "Philip deserves more than I can give him. That's why I'll have to give him up in the end." Her voice was steady and resolute.

"Oh, honey, don't make any major decisions. Take it one day at a time." Celia dabbed at her eyes with her napkin. "I wish I could give you better counsel than that, but frankly I'm at a loss. Ma's the one with all the wisdom in the family."

"I just needed someone to talk to. Someone who's known and shared my grief," Holly said. "Perhaps I somehow needed a Murphey's approval of my love affair, and I couldn't very well ask Grace for that. She'd be shocked."

"Oh, you'd be surprised how liberal Ma can be when it comes to affairs of the heart," Celia said. "Don't forget, she raised three daughters, and none of us were angels." She attempted a little smile. "Well, maybe *I* was."

"You?" Holly smiled back. "Don't forget, Ce, I once read your diary."

"That's right, you little demon." Celia's smile faded, and she became serious. "Holly, you don't need any Murphey approval for anything you do. It's your life, and we have no say in it. But I know I can speak for the entire family when I tell you that you'll always have our love and support."

Holly nodded. That's exactly what she'd needed to hear. She reached for Celia's hand and squeezed it.

"What's for dinner tomorrow?" Holly asked to lighten the mood, falling back on the tried-and-true Murphey joke about Grace's Sunday pot roast.

"Oh, I'm glad you reminded me, Hol. Get this. Ma's not making dinner for the gang tomorrow. She and Pa are going out to eat, instead."

It amazed Holly that she felt such relief. Until that moment she hadn't realized what a heavy obligation this weekly dinner had become to her. Not that the Murpheys had made it one. She had turned it into some kind of ritual to honor the memory of her husband and child.

Chapter Ten

I'm back, sweetheart."

"Oh, Philip, it's so good to hear your voice again!" Holly twirled, tangling the telephone cord around her body as she pressed the receiver against her ear.

"I've called you every day since I've been away," he reminded her.

"But now you're home. That makes all the difference in the world. I can't wait to see you."

"I can't wait to see you, either, Holly. But first I have to get King out of the kennel and clear up some work at the office. Can I pick you up around seven? We'll do something special to celebrate."

"Like what?"

"Oh, we'll think of something."

After Holly hung up, she placed her hand on her chest. She could feel her heart pounding hard. Philip had been gone for ten days, and each one had been longer than the next, an endless stretch of yearning. But it was over now. She'd be with him in less than two hours. Now that seemed as long as ten days. She decided to wear her new gray dress with the little white collar. Was it too prim? she worried. She smiled. The satin and lace undergarments she'd be wearing under it weren't prim at all.

Philip arrived ten minutes early, but Holly had been ready for thirty. When she threw open the door they stared at each other with frozen smiles on their faces for an uncomfortable moment, almost as if they were strangers. But in the next Philip swept her into his arms, and Holly felt more than physically close to him. Their hearts met. She pressed her cheek against his chest and breathed in his essence.

"Now I'm *really* home," he whispered, his fingers tangling in her hair. They stood together, simply holding each other, neither speaking.

"Let me look at you," Holly finally said, drawing away and tilting up her chin. Her eyes darted lovingly over each detail of his features. "Yes," she declared. "You look just the way I remembered you."

He pretended disappointment. "Not better?"

"Impossible!"

"And you..." He took her in with a head-to-toe glance and a pleased grin stretched his wide lips. "You look exactly as you did when you made those disturbing entrances into my dreams while I was away."

He embraced her again, and his lips sought hers. He kissed her roughly, greedily, then with a savoring gentleness that thrilled her even more. "How delicious you taste," he murmured. "Sweet as cotton candy. That's what we're having for dinner tonight, by the way."

"Cotton candy?" She laughed. Anything he could have said would have delighted her. His mere presence delighted her.

"And candied applies and snow cones and chili dogs."

"Oh, you're taking me to a health-food restaurant."

"No, sweetheart. I'm taking you to a carnival. I saw the Ferris wheel from the road as I was driving here. It looked like a beautiful, glittering mirage in the middle of a supermarket parking lot. I'm sure it's one of the first carnivals of the season. We don't want to miss it, do we?"

"Not for the world," Holly assured him. It happened to be one of her favorite entertainments.

"Then go pack a suitcase with all your essentials."

"Philip, I adore carnivals. But I'm not going to join up with one tonight."

"That's good, because I was hoping you'd spend the night with me." His eyes pleaded with her. "We have a lot of catching up to do, Holly. Please say you will. I promised King you would."

"Well, I wouldn't want to disappoint King."

"Great!" Philip grabbed her by the waist. "Oh, I can't wait to get you up on that Ferris wheel, sweetheart." He lifted her off her feet.

"No way," she said. "This is high enough for me, thank you. I'm afraid of heights, remember."

"Nonsense. A Ferris wheel is perfectly safe."

"I'll go on all the other rides with you," she said. "Even that torture machine that spins you around and turns you upside down. But *not* the Ferris wheel."

"We'll see." He put her down.

"I mean it, Philip."

He kissed her nose. "Go pack your bag," he said.

Like most of the couples there on Friday night dates, Holly and Philip strolled through the carnival hand in hand. It was a small affair organized by volunteer firemen to raise money for a charity. Holly had been to hundreds like it. But this one seemed magical to her. Philip seemed as enchanted as she. It was the first week of May, and spring saturated the mild night air. A full moon smiled down at them.

They stopped at each booth and tried their luck at games of chance. Philip refused to give up until he'd won a prize at each. Holly was now the proud owner of a plastic lei, a thick ballpoint pen that wrote in five different colors and a small rubber ball attached, for some indecipherable reason, to a key chain.

"Don't say I never bought you anything, sweetheart," Philip said after he'd presented her with the ball and key chain.

"And to think all these treasures only cost you fifty dollars, give or take a few tossed quarters."

"Oh, well, it's for charity. But I envy the lucky devil who wins that statue of the drunk hanging onto a lamppost. I had hoped to put it in my drawing room." He drawled the word.

"I don't think your decorator would approve, Philip."

"Really?" He looked shocked. "But the statue actually lights up, Holly!"

"Forget it," she said, tugging at his hand. "Let's go for a ride on the carousel."

"Or the Ferris wheel."

"You go. I'll stay on terra firma and wave up to you while you dangle in the air."

"That's no fun. You have to be sitting beside me so we can kiss and stuff when it stops at the top."

Holly arched an eyebrow. "And stuff?"

Philip's smile grew wider. "Just one of my teenage fantasies, Holly."

"You're thirty-eight," she reminded him.

"But I still drive a pickup truck, don't I?"

"Which I find rather endearing," she said. She stopped walking and gave him a quick kiss on the cheek.

They'd paused in front of another booth.

"Win the big teddy bear for your pretty lady, mister," the man behind it suggested. He was sporting a fireman's badge on his blazer.

The bear he pointed to was at least five feet tall and purple. Purple fuzz. It made Holly laugh. "Oh, I want that bear, Philip," she said.

"Then I'm going to get it for you, sweetheart."

"Easier said than done. We haven't been very lucky so far tonight."

"True. But those other games relied on chance. This one relies on skill." He eyed the ten clown heads lined up at the back of the booth. "How many do I have to knock down to win the bear?" he asked.

"All ten," the booth proprietor told him. "And you have to hit the clown directly on the nose to make it fall down."

"All ten!" Holly shook her head. "I don't think it can be done."

"O, ye of little faith!" Philip exclaimed. "It so happens I was the star pitcher of my high-school baseball team, Holly."

She'd already reminded him of his age and thought best not to remark that that had been twenty years ago.

But he must have seen the doubt in her face. "You really don't think I can do it, do you?"

She took his arm and turned him away. "Philip, I don't think anyone can do it," she said sotto voce. "These booths are set up to raise money, not to give away big prizes."

"I can do it," he insisted. "Listen, Holly. If I win that bear for you, will you go on the Ferris wheel with me?"

She sighed. "All right. Give it a try."

"I may need more than one," he hedged.

"Now wait a minute. How many tries are we talking about here? Five? Ten? A hundred?"

"You call it, Holly. Whatever you think is fair."

"Three is fair," she decided. "No more, no less."

"Oh, you're tough, sweetheart." He squeezed her arm. "But I accept the challenge."

Philip turned to the booth and laid down his money. ''Kiss that bear goodbye,'' he told the fireman confidently, picking up the first ball.

He knocked six clowns down before missing. He got seven on his second try. ''I'm all warmed up now,'' he said, slapping down another bill.

The man behind the booth looked a little nervous. ''Why not quit while you're ahead, mister? You've already won a chewable wax harmonica and a press-on tattoo kit.''

''Keep them! All I want is the bear.'' Philip took off his camel sweater, gave it to Holly and rolled up the sleeves of his blue chambray shirt. The man handed him another ball.

Holly stepped back to admire the way Philip wound up before he threw. Rather, she admired his strong, wide shoulders and muscular torso. She admired his intense determination, too. But she still didn't want to go on the Ferris wheel. After he'd knocked down nine clowns she cleared her throat. ''I don't want to get you nervous or break your concentration or anything, Philip, but it's all or nothing now.''

''Thank you for pointing that out to me, Holly.'' He smiled to show how much he appreciated it. ''I happen to *thrive* under pressure. You've given me just the incentive I need.''

The next ball he threw cracked the tenth clown's nose, and it went down hard.

After whooping with triumph Philip apologized to the fireman. ''Sorry I broke the clown's nose.''

''No problem. We got replacements in back.'' The man sighed. ''Not that we'll be getting too many more customers now that you've won the main attraction." He reached up to get the bear off the top shelf.

"Wait!" Holly said. "Let it stay where it is. I really don't have much use for an oversize teddy bear."

Philip hugged her to him. "That's right. She's already got me."

They strolled away before the flabbergasted fireman could thank them.

"Whether you took it or not, I still won that dumb bear for you, Holly." Philip pulled her toward the Ferris wheel. "And a deal's a deal."

"I'll go through with it," Holly replied in a small voice. The closer they got to the looming Ferris wheel, though, the tighter her stomach muscles became.

Philip bought the tickets, and they stood in line. Their turn came sooner than Holly wanted it to. The man operating the ride was very old, with hunched shoulders and shaky hands.

"Right this way, miss," he said, ushering her toward a waiting gondola.

She stepped back rather than forward. "What happens if this thing should start spinning out of control?" she asked him.

He cackled. "Never has, so I don't rightly know."

"You don't know?" Prickles of fear studded Holly's skin. "Don't you have some kind of emergency plan in case it does?"

"It won't," he said curtly, irritably. "Are you boarding or what?"

Philip nudged her forward. "We're boarding," he said.

Once they were seated in the gondola the old man clicked the safety bar into place. He pulled a lever, and they rose.

"Philip, I don't like this. I don't like this at all," Holly told him, curling her fingers around the cold metal bar. She shivered.

"Are you cold?" Philip draped his sweater over her shoulders.

"I'm frightened!"

He wrapped his arm around her. "Just relax, sweetheart."

Holly took a deep breath and closed her eyes. Her stomach dipped as she felt the gondola rise higher. Then it stopped and gently swayed back and forth. "Where are we?" she asked. "At the very top?"

Philip chuckled. "Why don't you take a peek and find out?"

"No, thanks."

"Holly, are you going to keep your eyes closed through the entire ride?"

"Absolutely."

"But that's no fun, sweetheart." She could feel the soft pressure of his mouth against her lids. "Come on," he cajoled. "Open your eyes. Look up instead of down."

She cautiously raised her lids and squinted at the bright full moon. It seemed close enough to touch. Gritting her teeth, she lowered her head. The strings of gaudy lights below blurred through the screen of her eyelashes. She opened her eyes wider. How small the people milling around looked from this vantage point.

Philip hugged her closer. "Not so terrifying, is it?"

She relaxed a little. "It's not as terrifying as I remember it, anyway," she conceded. "I was four years old the last time I took a ride on a Ferris wheel with my brother. I screamed so hysterically that the operator stopped the wheel and made us get off—which was fine with me. But my poor brother was humiliated."

The wheel started turning, and as the gondola traveled down, Holly's stomach lurched again. In a rush of panic, she grabbed onto Philip's thigh and squeezed hard.

"Easy, sweetheart," he cautioned. "Or I'm going to start screaming myself."

"Sorry." She eased her grip but kept a hold on him as the gondola fell to earth. But before it crashed it went up again, and Holly laughed. "This is sort of... fun," she allowed. She released Philip's leg and cuddled against him. "You can kiss me and stuff if you'd like."

"The date of my dreams," he said.

And when his lips crushed hers, Holly imagined the wheel spinning faster and faster. But she wasn't the least bit afraid anymore.

They slept late Saturday morning, apparently much to King's consternation.

"How nice, a barking alarm clock," Holly murmured, warm and cozy in Philip's embrace.

He groaned, rolled away from her and got out of bed. "King's demanding his morning walk."

"I'll make breakfast while you walk him." She pushed herself up on her elbows and watched him stride across the room naked, big and powerful and self-assured. Awakening to such a sight pleased her enormously.

"You'll have to make it out of thin air, I'm afraid," Philip said. "I haven't had a chance to shop for groceries." He pulled a pair of briefs from his dresser drawer and put them on.

Holly let out a little sigh. "What you need is a wi—" She bit her lip. "A housekeeper, Philip."

"Is that what you think I need?" His eyes searched her face.

She kept it blank. "You'd better go see to King before he has a conniption, poor thing."

"Right." He grabbed a pair of jeans and a sweatshirt from the closet and quickly dressed. "After I walk him, we'll make plans for the rest of the day." He bent to kiss her cheek. "And tonight. Now that I have you here with me, Holly, I'm not going to let you go for the entire weekend." He grazed his lips across her temple. "Stay put. I want to find you just where you are when I return."

Left alone in the big, wide bed, Holly rolled over to Philip's side. They'd enjoyed a beautiful night together, and she'd found herself wishing that it could last forever. But now, in the clear light of morning, she reminded herself that their relationship would have to come to an end eventually.

She had no intention of spending the weekend with Philip. They were getting too involved as it was. Holly still thought it possible to keep her love for him under control, to set limits on it. Complete and unconditional love meant pain and loss to her. That terrified her.

She threw off the covers. She had no intention of lolling in bed, either. But she couldn't quite bring herself to get dressed. She was glad she'd remembered to pack her new robe. She threw it on, and the silken fabric against her bare body made her feel both luxurious and slightly decadent. It was a marvelous feeling. She had to smile at herself. She'd never imagined she would be in such a position—a woman having a mad love affair with someone as handsome and exciting as Philip. Or with anyone, for that matter. She'd loved Daniel for as long as she could remember and had always assumed that they'd marry, raise a family and live....

Holly's smile faded and she hurried downstairs, lifting her robe with one hand and gliding the other along the banister.

She foraged through Philip's kitchen cupboards for coffee. He was well supplied with dog food, she noted. But nothing else. She gave up trying to find coffee in his cupboards and looked in the refrigerator. Since the last time she'd checked its contents, the head of lettuce had turned completely brown, one tall bottle of beer was gone, but the three eggs and wedge of cheese remained. As did the ironstone baking dish containing what was once leftover lasagna. Holly didn't lift the aluminum covering to see what it had turned into.

She took out the three eggs, found a bowl and, holding her breath, cracked one egg into it. She dared a sniff, then, holding her breath again, poured it down the drain. She put the other two eggs aside very carefully, as if they were bombs ready to go off.

She decided that the freezer was safer territory. She discovered a can of coffee there. Eureka! And a package of blueberry turnovers. Double eureka!

When Philip returned with King, the coffee was perking and the turnovers were baking in the oven.

"I was hoping to find you still in bed," he said.

"After last night, we need fuel for the fire, darling."

Had Holly realized she'd called him darling? Philip wondered. As loving as she was in bed, she was short on endearments. As much as she gave to him physically, Philip sensed that she was understandably holding back on him. She had lost so much before. He'd be as patient as possible, but he wouldn't let her forget how much he wanted her. "Fuel for the fire?" he asked. "As far as I'm concerned, it's still raging. Maybe we should go upstairs and take a shower together."

Holly found his suggestion more than a little appealing. So appealing that she allowed him to take her hand and lead her upstairs.

As rustic as Philip's tower was, his bathroom was state-of-the-art modern. The large shower stall was a curving expanse of steel and Plexiglas. The sunken whirlpool tub was wide and deep.

Philip noted Holly giving the tub a covetous look. He turned on the faucets full blast. "It takes a while to fill."

"What could we possibly do in the meantime?" Holly asked sweetly.

"Let's start with this," he said in his low, quiet voice, parting her silk robe to unveil her breasts. He lowered his head and suckled them as the bathroom steamed up.

Holly clutched his thick head of hair as her limbs turned to jelly. He opened her robe to reveal her completely and trailed slow, lingering kisses along her smooth torso. Spanning her slender waist with his palms, he knelt down and rubbed his beard-roughened cheek against her satiny stomach.

Holly shivered with delight and laughed. "You need a shave, darling." She slid down beside him and stroked his cheek. "Let me do it." The suggestion surprised her, but the moment it popped out of her mouth, she liked the idea.

Philip looked doubtful. "Have you ever shaved a man before?"

"No, but I'm sure I can manage it." She pulled him up with her. "First you have to take off all your clothes."

"That's not how they do it at the barbershop."

"I should hope not!" She went to the cabinet and took out his old-fashioned soap mug and brush and razor with a curved horn handle. When she turned back, he'd already undressed. Noting his arousal, Holly's eyes sparkled wickedly. "Now get into the tub and relax, Philip. This is going to be fun."

"Fun? Why do I feel like a guinea pig?" he muttered, but he did as he was told. He shut off the rushing faucets. "Do you want me to turn on the whirlpool?"

"Not quite yet." Holly placed his shaving equipment at the edge of the tub and slipped off her robe, enjoying Philip's undivided attention. It fell from her body and puddled around her feet. She tested the water with her big toe.

"Just the right temperature," she pronounced.

Did Holly know how breathtaking she looked right now? Philip guessed she probably did. That's why she was taking her sweet time about getting into the tub and driving him crazy in the process. She reminded him of a water sprite poised at the edge of some magical pond—so slender yet sensual, with her glossy cap of hair, small, perfectly shaped breasts, tapering waist and long, shapely legs. She was a goddess, all right. *His* goddess.

"Are you going to join me or tease me all morning?" he asked gruffly, embarrassed by his complete adoration of her.

"Both!" she declared, stepping into the warm water. She slowly lowered herself into it. "Ooh," she sighed. "Delightful." Her breasts bobbed just above the surface.

Philip reached for her but, quick as a playful otter, she eluded him. "Shave and a haircut, two bits!" she sang out, reaching for the mug and brush.

"I don't think this is such a good idea, sweetheart."

"What?" She pretended a pout. "You promised you'd let me, Philip."

Desire clouded his better judgment. "Hell, you can shave my whole body if you want to," he allowed.

"Oh, no. I like your body just the way it is." She swirled the soft bristle brush across his shoulders and hairy chest, circling each nipple, then along his flat stomach, circling his navel. She smiled when his muscles tightened with a quick intake of breath. She dipped the brush lower and he groaned as she stroked his most sensitive area with it. He made an attempt to grab her again but she'd expected it and slipped away.

"Now, Philip, let's concentrate on your *face*."

She dipped the brush in the mug and twirled it around until the soap became frothy. Kneeling between Philip's legs, she dabbed his face with it. His eyes never left her bobbing breasts.

She leaned back to examine his foamy white beard. "What a sexy Santa you'd make," she told him.

"Holly, I'm begging you. Just get on with this, okay?"

"Okay," she blithely agreed, picking up the razor. "So where do I start?"

Philip raised his eyes to heaven. "I must be crazy, letting you do this. Talk about being a fool for love!"

"I appreciate your trust in me, Philip." She lowered the razor and kissed him on the mouth instead, then leaned back on her haunches and smiled through the foam around her own lips. "I would never take the chance of nicking you. I would never chance hurting you in the slightest way," she told him.

Philip released a sigh of relief. "I was going to let you have your way with me, you know."

"Oh, I still intend to do that, my darling man." She kissed him again and again, all over his soapy face, until hers was almost as soapy.

His deep, pleased laughter ricocheted off the tiles.

By the time they'd dried themselves off, dressed and gone downstairs, the blueberry turnovers had burned to a crisp in the oven. Holly removed the charred remains and shook her head.

"If we continue this affair, Philip, we're both going to starve to death."

If? Affair? Even though he realized that Holly was joking, Philip didn't like the sound of that one bit. He poured himself a cup of coffee, yanked out a chair, sat down at the table and frowned.

Taking in Philip's expression, Holly concluded that hunger had put him out of sorts. He'd certainly been in high enough spirits upstairs in his bathtub.

"Unless we want to dig into King's food supply, we'll have to go out for breakfast," she said.

"Fine."

"And then I'd like you to take me home. I really can't spend the weekend here. We both have our own lives to lead and—"

"Fine!" Philip said again, much louder.

King, who'd been curled at his feet, sat up and looked at Philip with as much surprise as Holly did.

"Why are you shouting?" she asked.

"Why are you always so damn elusive?" he boomed. "You give me everything I'd always hoped for from a woman when we make love, then you want to leave. You always want to leave!"

Holly said nothing.

Philip's broad shoulders sagged as he hunched over his coffee cup. He didn't want to chance losing her. "All right, Holly. I'll take you home if that's what you want."

"Yes, that's what I want," she said, lying through her teeth as she stiffly smiled at him. It was for the best, she told herself.

They stopped at a highway fast-food chain on the way to New Haven. Their polite conversation was as artificial as the food they consumed. When Philip double-parked in front of Holly's apartment house he offered to bring up her suitcase for her. She told him it wasn't necessary and got out. She waved as he sped off, but he didn't wave back.

She'd warned him, Philip reminded himself as he headed toward the highway. Holly had warned him that she would set boundaries around her heart. He had no right to be angry with her now. He was more upset than angry. Why couldn't she just let herself go and be *happy* with him, dammit?

He appreciated how her tragic loss had made her feel vulnerable. Some people never recovered from a loss like that. Yet Philip truly believed that Holly's inner spirit was resilient, indomitable. She hadn't lost her capacity to feel joy. She'd only suppressed it. He knew this because he could see that joyous spirit in her crystalline eyes when she looked at him, he could feel it in her touch, hear it in her voice. She was a giving, loving woman. He didn't for a moment consider that this was only wishful thinking on his part. Once Philip believed in something or someone, he never had second thoughts. He'd always trusted his heart and instincts.

That's what Holly had to learn how to do again, he decided. And she would. He was sure of it. He'd help her let go of her pain and let herself love again. She would eventually release the tight rein she kept on her spirits and let them soar like a big, bright balloon. Philip grinned. He'd just thought of a perfect adventure for her. But would she go along with it? His grin widened with confidence. He'd gotten her up on that Ferris wheel, hadn't he?

Chapter Eleven

The doorbell rang sharply. Holly stumbled out of bed and looked out the window. Philip's shiny green truck glinted in the early morning sunlight. She hurried to the door to let him in.

"Did I wake you?" he asked. He was dressed in his black sweatshirt, jeans and running shoes.

Holly dragged a hand through her sleep-tousled hair. "Considering that it's the crack of dawn, that's a pretty good assumption."

"The sun's been up for at least an hour."

"Philip, it's an unwritten law in all civilized societies that you never visit people before ten on a Sunday morning." She wished she were wearing her new lace nightgown instead of a baggy, rumpled sleep shirt.

"Aren't you happy to see me, sweetheart?"

"Yes, I'm happy to see you," she admitted, wrapping her arms around his waist. He smelled like sunshine and fresh air. "I tossed and turned all night, knowing you were angry with me."

"I wasn't angry. Just disappointed that you wouldn't stay with me." He stroked her back as she hugged him. "Oh, you feel so good. I'm tempted to take you right back to bed."

Holly nestled closer against him to demonstrate that she wouldn't object.

But Philip sighed and stepped away. "We've got to stay on schedule, though. Go get dressed, Holly. I suggest jeans and a warm sweater. It's mild out, but it can get a little nippy where we're going."

"Where *are* we going?"

"I can't tell you that. It'll ruin the surprise."

"I don't like surprises."

"You'll like this one," he assured her.

"At least give me a hint."

"Okay. We're going as close to heaven as possible."

She laced her arms around his neck and gave him a devilish smile. "You've already taken me there without even leaving bed. So why don't we just stay here all morning?"

He chuckled. "Holly Murphey, how you talk. I'd never guess you were the same reserved lady I met at Jerome Academy not too long ago." He gave her backside a pat. "But I'm not going to let you seduce me now. People are waiting for us."

She untwined her hands from his neck and shook his shoulders. "Tell me, Philip. What people? Where?"

"The sooner you get dressed, the faster you'll find out."

Giving a cry of frustration, she headed for her bedroom to do just that. She decided to wear the red sweater she'd bought during her shopping spree with Celia. As she was slipping it on over her jeans, it hit her. Today was Sunday, which meant dinner at the Murpheys. How could she have possibly forgotten?

"I have to be in Milford no later than noon today, Philip," she told him when she returned to the living room

"What? Impossible. I can never get you back by then."

"Then I can't go with you. I always have dinner with the Murphey family on Sunday."

Disappointment darkened his gray eyes. "That's your choice, of course."

And Holly understood that it was an important choice. She could relive her past happiness with the Murpheys today or enjoy the present with Philip.

"I'll call and tell them I can't make it today," she said. She went to her bedroom and closed the door behind her.

Philip sank down on the sofa and exhaled a deep, long breath. He recognized the importance of Holly's decision as much as she did. Not only had she agreed to break an established pattern from the past and come with him. She'd agreed without even knowing where he was taking her! Did she realize what a step toward a future together that was? he mused. Even if she didn't realize it, she'd made that first step, as far as he was concerned.

Holly dialed the Murpheys' number, knowing Mike always rose at dawn. He answered on the second ring.

"Good morning, Mike."

"Holly! How ya doing, honey? Missed your pretty face last week."

"Did you enjoy your dinner at the inn last Sunday?"

"Let me tell you, it was a *beauteeful* buffet. Fish, meats, casseroles, desserts. You name it, they had it. Except pot roast. No pot roast in sight."

Holly laughed. "When I talked to Grace last week she said you were like a kid in a candy shop."

"Yeah, but I couldn't handle it more than once a month, or I'd get fatter than I already am. That's what Gracie and I decided. We'll eat there once a month now. The other three Sundays, it's dinner at the Murpheys' as usual."

"Except I'm not going to be there as usual today, Mike."

"You sick?" Concern immediately entered his voice.

"I've never felt better. Actually, Mike, I have a..." She couldn't do it. She couldn't bring herself to tell Daniel's father that she had a date with a man. "I have a lot of work to do. Exams and compositions to correct."

"So the teacher has to catch up on *her* homework for a change," Mike joked. "I understand, and so will Grace. Just don't work too hard, okay, honey?"

"Okay." Holly hung up feeling terribly guilty. But she hadn't really lied, she told herself. In fact she did have a lot of paperwork to clear up before classes tomorrow. She hadn't been able to concentrate all day Saturday after parting with Philip so coolly.

She plucked the goddess off her night table, tucked it into her jeans pocket and went back to Philip. "I'm all set to go with you now, Philip," she announced. "Wherever *that* might be."

He smiled. "If there's one thing I love, it's a woman with a sense of adventure, sweetheart."

"Then you've picked the wrong one!"

"I don't think so." His smile never wavered.

Even before she noticed the cars parked in the open field, Holly saw IT in the distance—a massive blue-and-yellow striped balloon lying on its side like a beached whale. So that was Philip's surprise! She wanted no part of it.

"No way," she said. "Absolutely not. Forget it, Philip. Turn your truck around and take me home immediately."

He stopped instead and turned off the motor. "You're going to love it, Holly. Trust me."

"Ha!" She glared at him. "I trusted you enough to be tricked like this. You know how I feel about heights."

"That's what you said about the Ferris wheel, but you ended up enjoying the ride, didn't you?"

"Ferris wheels are stationary objects. Balloons go up, up, up!" Her voice went up a few octaves, too. "There's no controlling them!"

"The pilot controls the altitude," Philip explained patiently. "And I have a balloon pilot's license. So there's nothing to worry about, Holly. The conditions are perfect today."

"Not my condition, Philip. My heart is pounding, my palms are sweaty, and I'm not budging from this truck."

"The moment we're aloft, your fears will pass," he assured her.

"I'd just as soon pass up the experience, thank you."

Philip got out, walked around the truck and opened her door. "At least take a look at the balloon close up. It's my pride and joy. And I want you to meet my ground crew. I told them you were coming."

Holly could see the six-member team milling around IT. "All right, Philip. I'll go look at your balloon. I'll even admire it. But I will not, I repeat *not*, go up in it with you."

"We'll see," he said mildly.

Holly hopped out of the cab, deciding to humor him since he'd gone to so much trouble. She would humor him up to a point. And that point ended on solid ground. Her feet would never leave it, she assured herself as she walked across the field with him. Yet her heart continued to beat faster than normal.

Philip hooked her arm with his. "This field is where I'm going to build my next condo project," he told her. "Prime location. Within commuting distance to both New Haven and Stamford."

"Sounds perfect," Holly said. "You'll be able to get top dollar for the units."

"I don't want to get top dollar for the units, Holly. I want them to be affordable to the average family starting out. Look over there."

He pointed in the distance. Holly saw nothing but leveled land.

"That's where the green's going to be," Philip told her. "A park and playground. No fancy pool or tennis courts. Just a safe green place where neighbors can gather and kids can run wild. Each unit will face the green, so everybody can keep an eye on the kids. I want to bring back a sense of community, Holly. A sense of neighborhood."

She pressed her cheek against his shoulder. "I like the concept."

"It's hardly a new one. But it's one that developers in this area have ignored for the past few decades. No one's building middle-income housing anymore. Single family homes are getting bigger and bigger because land is so expensive. And most of the condominiums around here restrict children."

"Then you'll definitely fill a need with this project."

"Tell my board of directors and investors and financial advisers that! It amazes me that I can't get the support I need. But even if I don't, I'm going to go through with this project."

Holly admired him for his conviction. She had to admire his tenacity, too. Or was it plain old-fashioned stubbornness? Whatever it was, it had made him a success. As they came closer to the balloon, she could see the name Irons, Inc. emblazoned across it in bold white letters. Two crew members held open the mouth of the balloon as another directed a motor-driven fan into it to fill it with air.

Philip waved to the crew chief directing the procedure and motioned her over. "Carol Burke, this is Holly Murphey. Holly has a few misgivings about flying with me."

Carol took off her thick gloves and shook Holly's hand. "You've got nothing to worry about, Holly. Phil's a great pilot. He taught me everything I know."

"Did he?" Holly forced a smile. Carol wasn't just pretty. Her flashing brown eyes and blond hair made her exceptionally so.

"Yeah, thanks to him I earned my student pilot certificate last month. Take it from me, you're in good hands with Phil."

Holly found herself wishing that Carol's eyes didn't twinkle quite so much when she said that. "It's not Philip's ability I'm worried about," she said.

Carol gave her an understanding nod. "You're scared. Listen, so was I the first time I went up in a balloon. Of course, I was only ten at the time." Giving Holly an encouraging slap on the back, she turned to Philip. "All set for you to activate the burner, Phil."

"Let me have a few minutes alone with Holly first, okay?"

"Sure." Carol shook a finger at her. "Now don't you chicken out," she said in parting.

"Don't let Carol pressure you, sweetheart," Philip said, taking Holly into his arms. "I don't want you to fly with me if you don't really want to. You can meet me at the landing sight with the ground crew, instead.

But I promise you that if you come up with me, you're going to love it."

He exuded such confidence that Holly found herself believing him. When she was with him, she had a tendency to believe that anything and everything was possible. "You're tempting me," she admitted.

"That's exactly what I'm trying to do. Come up on my magic carpet with me, sweetheart. There's nothing to fear."

"But fear itself," she added, lifting her chin. "You may not believe this, Philip, but I used to be quite a daredevil in my day."

"Oh, I believe it."

"So what are we waiting for?" She tugged *him* along as she marched to the balloon. Still, she eyed the supine giant suspiciously. "How are you going to get it upright?"

"Easy. Just heat the air."

Philip turned off the fan, activated the burner and cracked open the blast valve. The resulting flame shot heat into the balloon, and it slowly rose, lifting the basket upright. He hopped in, checked his equipment and instruments carefully, made sure the vents were closed, sealing the balloon, and set the altimeter.

"Come aboard, Holly. We're all set to go."

It was her last chance to back out. But she knew that if she did, she would always regret it. When she was old and gray she would think back to this sunny day in May and either smile fondly at the memory or sadly shake her head over her lack of adventure. She scrambled into the basket.

"Onward and upward!" she said with more bravado than she felt.

"That's the spirit." Philip turned on the blast valve again, and the basket began to lift off the ground. Holly experienced a surge of panic but quelled it by holding onto Philip's arm. Smiling bravely, she waved to the crew below. They got smaller and smaller as the balloon rose higher and higher.

Except for the short, occasional bursts from the burner, which controlled the vertical direction of the balloon, there was only quiet as they floated through the sky. Total peace. Unlike the Ferris wheel gondola, the basket didn't sway.

"I've located an air mass moving in the right direction and hitched a ride on it," Philip told her. "Look how the world slides by beneath us." He stood behind Holly and wrapped his arms around her waist.

Feeling safe in the circle of his strong arms, she leaned over the basket and looked down. It seemed as if someone was pulling the earth out from under their feet. Oddly enough, Holly wasn't the least bit disturbed by this extraordinary sensation.

"It's out of a dream," she sighed. "I used to have this wonderful dream that I was soaring through the sky of my own volition." She didn't mention that she'd stopped having that dream after losing her husband and child.

They slowly glided over the suburban terrain of highways and shopping centers and housing developments and towns, spotted by patches of farmland and woods and golf courses. They were traveling in a southwest direction, and to their left Long Island

Sound looked like a big blue puddle decorated with toy sailboats.

"Let's have a little fun," Philip said when they passed over another golf course. He let the balloon dip lower and lower, since there was no danger of it tangling with power lines. "Hang on," he cautioned as the basket skimmed over the tops of a clump of maple trees. And then they descended even lower, until they were less than ten feet from the ground.

A golf cart came to a sudden stop, and two men jumped out to watch the balloon approach, mouths hanging open. They couldn't have looked more amazed if it had been a spacecraft.

"Just passing through," Philip shouted. Holly blew them a kiss.

They continued floating above the emerald expanse until they reached a foursome with caddies. Everybody smiled up at them and waved.

"Take me! Take me back with you!" one of the young caddies yelled. "I saw *Close Encounters* ten times!"

"I'll send E.T. to pick you up," Philip promised.

"Wrong movie, man!" the caddie shouted, dropping the bag of clubs he was carrying and running alongside the basket. "And forget E.T. I want your friend in the red sweater to pick me up."

Holly, laughing, blew him a kiss, too. Philip shot some hot air into the balloon and made it rise. "Fresh kid," he growled, leaving him behind.

They descended again and headed for another male foursome.

"Why aren't there any women on this course?" Holly asked.

"None allowed, sweetheart. This happens to be the most exclusive country club in Connecticut."

"How terribly, terribly stuffy," she said, talking through her nose.

"That's why they need a balloon visitation."

As Philip and Holly sailed toward the golfers, three of them looked up and waved. But the golfer about to tee off raised his club and pointed it at them like a gun. "Interlopers!" he cried. "This is private property, for members only! You and that *female* don't belong here. Get out!"

"Hey, you don't own the air space, you old codger."

"Intolerable," the man boomed back. "I'm going to voice a complaint directly to your boss, young man. My brother happens to be on the board of directors of Mr. Irons's corporation."

"Have a heart, sir," Holly pleaded, leaning over the basket. "Please don't tell Mr. Irons. He's a very severe man, devoid of humor, much like you are. He'll surely fire us."

"Good!" the man shouted back, waving his golf club at her as the balloon drifted up into the clouds.

Philip dug his fingers under the waistband of Holly's jeans and pulled her away from the edge of the basket.

"Forget that pompous fool, Holly. Why'd you put on an act for him?"

"Because I didn't want him to guess that you were Mr. Irons."

"I don't give a damn if he does."

"Didn't you say you were having trouble with your board of directors about your latest project? So why ruffle feathers? The idea of this balloon is to promote your company, not alienate potential investors."

"I didn't realize you were so savvy about high finance, Holly."

She laughed at that. "To me high finance is balancing my checkbook. I'm just talking common sense, Philip."

"And that ain't hot air, sweetheart," he said, turning on the valve to shoot some more into the balloon. "But you have to admit that this is a great idea of mine for promoting the company."

"He said modestly," Holly murmured.

"Deep down I'm really very humble," Philip told her.

"Ha! Unpretentious, perhaps. But certainly not humble."

"My beginnings were. Remind me to tell you the story of my life one of these days, Holly."

"Now's as good a time as any."

"No, I don't want to distract you from enjoying the scenery." He encircled her waist from behind again, sliding cool fingers beneath her sweater to stroke her smooth, flat stomach.

His cool touch produced a radiating warmth within her, and she leaned against his chest. "What you're doing now is pretty distracting."

"I can't help it. I love touching you." He pressed her even closer against him. "You know, Holly, you could make the story of my life complete. I'd like you to share the rest of it with me."

Philip felt her stomach muscles tense beneath his fingers. He hadn't intended to tell her that. Rather, he'd intended to wait a little longer before he did. But he'd never been one to bide his time when he wanted something badly. He'd never been good at dissembling.

"Please, Philip. Let's not talk about the rest of our lives. Let's simply cherish what we have now before it slips away." Holly turned and kissed him deeply, hoping he would understand that counting on anything but the present moment filled her with trepidation.

His mouth claimed hers possessively as he crushed her against him, and she could sense he wanted to claim her very heart and soul. While they embraced, they felt a deep shuddering as the balloon passed through air masses moving in opposite directions.

Philip raised his mouth from hers. "That was just a wind shear," he said, gazing into her translucent blue eyes. He saw love in them, pure and simple, and told himself that that was enough. For now.

They continued on their floating journey above the earth, seemingly at peace with each other. But Holly knew that Philip would never be satisfied with keeping their relationship in abeyance, suspended midair like the balloon, drifting without a purpose. As much as he liked heights, he needed a firm base to build on. And he needed a woman with whom to build a future.

"There's Jennings Beach up ahead," he said, breaking into her thoughts. "Our landing site."

"Now that I'm up, I don't want to go down," Holly told him with deep regret in her voice. "But all good things must come to an end eventually."

"Oh, don't look so sad," Philip said, chucking her chin. "I'll take you up any time you want. I'll even teach you how to fly."

Holly shook her head. "I don't have the heart for it."

"Sure you do," Philip insisted. "You're as fearless as they come, Holly. You just don't realize it."

He would always refuse to see her limitations, Holly realized. That was Philip's way. "For someone who's supposed to be so fearless," she said, "I'm getting awfully anxious about landing."

"All you have to do is face the direction of travel. When the basket makes impact with the ground, bend your knees slightly. And don't climb out until I tell you to. Got that?"

She nodded solemnly.

"The wind's picked up a little bit, so the balloon may act like a sail and drag the basket through the sand for a few yards. I don't think that's going to happen, but I wanted you to be prepared."

"I won't panic," she assured him.

"I know you won't, sweetheart." He grinned and gave her a peck on the cheek.

They were directly above the large expanse of beach now, and Holly could see the ground crew gathered in the parking lot. When the balloon descended to the proper elevation, Philip turned off the blast valve and pulled the deflation line. A large panel of the balloon opened, and it began to descend much more rapidly. The crew began running toward them and so did some strollers on the beach. As Holly held her breath, the basket made a soft, perfect landing on the sand.

"Amazing!" she cried, giving Philip a joyous hug.

"Nothing to it," he replied. "A piece of cake." He swung her out of the basket.

The moment Holly's feet touched the sand she began dancing, elated. Life could be so wonderful, she thought. She beamed at Philip, who was climbing out of the basket.

"I love you," she said.

Her declaration made Philip pause in midaction, and at that moment a gust of wind caused the balloon to sail forward, tilting the basket before he'd made his way free of it. He fell backward and the basket overturned on his leg.

Holly screamed and ran to help him, throwing her weight against the basket to push it back. It was a futile gesture. The basket was far too heavy. Luckily, the crew arrived and heaved it upright again.

"Don't move," Holly enjoined, kneeling in the sand beside Philip and placing her trembling hands on his shoulders. "Something may be broken."

"That's a definite possibility," Philip said, wincing with pain.

King didn't know what to make of the plaster cast on Philip's leg. When Philip and Holly first entered the tower, the dog barked furiously. Holly tried to calm him as Philip hobbled across the room, but the sight of his master on crutches sent King into a tailspin.

"It's okay, pal," Philip said, easing himself down on the sofa. "Come here and give me a lick."

But King kept his distance for a good ten minutes, hovering in the corner of the big room, whimpering. He finally edged closer, tail drooping, and extended his neck to sniff the cast, which sheathed Philip's left leg from knee to ankle. Philip wiggled his toes, and King drew back.

"Better get used to it," Philip said, laughing. "I'm going to be wearing it for the next few weeks."

"The doctor said six to ten," Holly reminded him, fluffing up a pillow and putting it behind his back.

"Yeah, but I'm a fast healer. It's just a simple fracture, and it's a lucky thing I broke my fibula instead of my tibia."

Holly sighed deeply and her breath came out ragged. "You really are the perennial optimist, darling."

"Listen, I consider this a very lucky day," he insisted. "Today Holly Murphey told me she loved me."

She sank down beside him. "Oh, Philip, if I hadn't distracted you, you would have climbed out of the basket before it tilted over. It's all my fault!" For the past few hours she'd been consumed by that thought.

"That's ridiculous," Philip told her sternly. "You had nothing to do with it. A gust of wind made the basket tilt. Do you think you conjured it up with your words?"

She could almost believe she had. She had tempted the fates by daring to love Philip. She'd exposed her heart to their whims even though she'd promised herself never to let that happen again.

"But I *distracted* you," she repeated. "If only I hadn't—"

"Sweetheart, you weren't responsible," Philip interrupted. "Why do you insist on blaming yourself?"

She covered her face with her hands and shook her head. Philip's accident had aroused so many deep-seated, tormenting feelings and memories. She'd been consumed by guilt four years before, blaming herself for her husband and child's accident because she'd bought them skates for Christmas. If only, if only, if only...that had been the constant chant beating in her breast for months.

She became aware of Philip's hand on her hunched back, stroking her, comforting her. She should be comforting him! But she couldn't. She couldn't look at him now. She pushed herself off the sofa and hurried to the kitchen area.

"I'm going to make you some tea," she said, wiping the tears from her eyes as she filled the kettle. She put it on the stove and checked his refrigerator. "And then I'm going to go buy you some groceries." She hoped he didn't notice that her voice was shaky as she called to him. "And then I'm going to cook you dinner." The trick was to keep busy, she knew. It had always saved her in the past.

"Hey, I'm not an invalid!" Philip protested.

"Well, you're not about to run a marathon, either," she replied. She took a deep breath, waited a moment and, feeling she had her emotions under control, came back to stand before him, hands on her hips. "Honestly, Philip, I don't know why you insist on staying in this tower while your leg's in a cast. I'll be happy to move all your things into a bedroom in the main part of the house. Then you won't have all those stone steps to deal with every day."

"Holly, I like it here. King likes it here. The rest of the house is for business, but the tower is my home."

"And a very fine home it is," she replied, trying to humor him. "For a man with two working legs."

"I climbed up here on crutches just fine, didn't I?"

His agility had impressed her, but she thought best not to tell him that now. "You haven't tried climbing *down*, though."

"The challenge appeals to me." His ruddy face took on a stubborn set.

"Philip, please listen to reason. The doctor told you to remain as immobile as possible. I was sitting right there in the office with you when he said that. Oh, that reminds me. You have to take one of those painkillers now."

"I don't need any drugs to get me through."

"Stop being such a baby."

"A baby? I'm hanging tough here, Holly."

"You're taking your medication, and that's final. I'll go get you a glass of water."

Philip wasn't sure if he found comfort in Holly's bossy tone or resented it. A little of both, he decided. He thought he'd be the one helping her today. Yet as much as he wanted to be in control at all times, he wanted to be cared for, too. Besides, whether he was willing to admit it to her or not, he *was* in pain at the moment. Not a lot. But not a little, either. He dug into the pocket of his jeans and fished out the envelope of tablets the doctor had given him. The left pant leg had been split to accommodate his bulky cast.

"It took one second for my fibula bone to break," he said when Holly returned. "But it took years to break in these jeans. These were my favorite jeans of all, Holly."

"Poor darling."

She gave him a kiss of commiseration on the forehead and hovered over him as he swallowed the pill. Then she scurried across the room again to answer the kettle's whistle. By the time she returned with Philip's cup of tea, she was wishing that his tower was a lot smaller.

She sat beside him and attempted to reason with him once again. "Philip, how are you going to maneuver that treacherous metal stairway up to your bedroom?"

"No problem."

"But it's definitely a problem. Please admit it, darling, and move to one of the bedrooms in the main part of the mansion."

"I'm not going to let a little thing like a broken leg disturb my life-style, dammit!"

Holly didn't find his stubbornness so charming at the moment. She found it downright infuriating. "One slip and you may end up with *two* broken legs, Philip. Why can't you be sensible about this?"

"Don't worry about me, Holly. I'll be fine."

Why were men so difficult when they were injured or sick? Holly wondered. Well, she couldn't force him to do something he didn't want to do. She got up and grabbed her purse and the keys to his truck. "I'll go get some groceries," she said. "What would you like for dinner?"

"A nice big juicy steak."

"Which you'll probably eat raw, macho man," she murmured.

"Hey, I'm not trying to be macho. This tower is my retreat. Can't you understand that, Holly?"

"Yes," she said softly. She understood all about retreating.

An hour later, when Holly returned with the groceries, she found Philip dozing on the sofa. She gazed down at his sleeping face, and her heart filled with love. He opened his eyes, and she knelt beside him.

"How do you feel?" she asked, stroking his hair.

"Groggy. I knew I shouldn't have taken that pill."

"Philip, I've decided to spend the night here if you don't mind," she said.

"Mind?" He grinned and touched her cheek. "I want you to spend *every* night with me, sweetheart."

"No, just tonight. I want to make sure you can manage those stairs on your own. I'll have to borrow your truck to get to New Haven tomorrow morning."

"Jack can drive you there. He can bring you back to Fairfield tomorrow evening, too. Unless you prefer using your own car."

"Tomorrow? Philip, I'm only spending tonight here."

"We'll see."

Holly knew by now that when Philip said "we'll see" he really meant "we'll see things my way in the end." But she had no intention of moving in with him until his cast was removed. If he insisted on staying in the tower, he would have to manage on his own. She certainly wasn't going to accommodate his stubbornness. Absolutely not.

Chapter Twelve

By midweek Holly had become accustomed to commuting from Fairfield to New Haven every morning. She'd park close to her apartment and walk to the diner to have breakfast with Mr. Brakenbiddle as usual. After work she'd stop by her apartment to feed her goldfish, check her mail and telephone answering machine and to get clothes for the next day. Then she would drive to Fairfield. She kept telling herself that she would spend only one more night with him. She'd been telling herself this for three days now.

When Philip came to the tower from his office on the other side of the mansion Wednesday, Holly was already in the kitchen starting dinner.

"Hi, sweetheart, I'm home," he said.

The comforting familiarity of the greeting made her heart squeeze tight. They were already falling into domestic habits that she knew would be extremely difficult to break.

"Something smells delicious," Philip said, making his way toward her on his crutches.

"Chicken paprika," she told him, meeting him halfway and hugging him. She treasured the sight and feel of him. "I'm making enough for you to warm up tomorrow since I won't be here for dinner."

"Why? Do you have a late meeting at school?"

"No, Philip. But I can't keep coming every night. You can manage on your own."

"Of course I can," he readily agreed.

Holly knew that he wasn't taking her seriously. Why should he? She'd been telling him she wasn't coming back since the beginning of the week. But she really meant it this time. He'd proven beyond a shadow of a doubt that he could manage all the flights of stairs quite easily.

That night they read together in Philip's big bed like an established married couple. Holly treasured the easy intimacy of it. At the same time she longed to make love with him.

"How's your leg?" she asked casually, turning a page of her romance novel.

"It itches like crazy," he said, swatting at the cast with his paperback detective novel. "But the pain's disappeared."

"Well, that's good. I would never dream of taking advantage of a man in pain." She threw aside her book and lightly ran her fingers through his rough chest hair.

"Would you consider taking advantage of a man with a cast on his leg, though?" he asked.

She let her lips toy with his ear before replying. And then she whispered into it. "It's been my favorite fantasy lately."

"What a coincidence," he said in a thick voice. "I've been having this fantasy about a blue-eyed woman with dark, silky hair and the most delightfully perky breasts taking advantage of *me*."

"Perhaps we could share our fantasies," she softly suggested.

"Well, mine starts out just this way," Philip replied, pushing aside the thin fabric of her nightgown to touch her breasts. "And then, because the poor man is a little restricted in his movements, the woman leans over him . . ."

Holly adjusted her position. "Like this?"

"Oh, yes. Exactly like that." He continued to fondle her breasts as he suckled them.

She felt the pull of desire, the melting need for more, but drew away to tease him, to tantalize him. "Then what happens?" she asked in a whispery voice.

Philip's eyes glinted with desire and impatience. "Then the man rips off his cast with his bare hands to discover that his leg has magically mended. He throws the willing lady down and makes mad, passionate love to her, satisfying her completely."

"I have an even better fantasy, darling," Holly said, stripping off her nightgown. "Since the man isn't about to tear off his cast in reality, the lady takes over. If the man is up to it, that is."

"*Up* to it!" Philip glowered, offended. "Obviously he is."

Holly glided her hand down Philip's muscular body. "Obviously," she agreed. Slowly, ever so slowly, she pulled his striped pajama bottoms off and straddled him carefully. "We don't want to jostle that poor, broken leg of yours, do we?" she said, guiding him into her.

"Jostle all you like, sweetheart," he sighed. "All I can feel now is total pleasure."

"I'll still be gentle with you," she assured him.

Holly had never felt so in control and yet uninhibited as she made love to Philip this way. His passion-glazed eyes worshiped her as she moved above him, and she smiled down at him with sensual delight. Watching his face change expression with every nuance of her movements doubled her pleasure as she pleasured him.

"How beautiful you are," he said, molding her slender curves with his palms. "How I love looking at you." He massaged her taut abdomen with strong, knowing fingers, his thumbs circling lower and lower. Holly arched above him and moaned. "Oh, yes, I love looking at you like this," he said.

She reveled in his adoration. It made her bold and confident. She leaned forward to kiss him deeply, then leaned back again to slow the rhythm of their embrace. She wanted their lovemaking to last for as long as possible, until neither of them could bear it a moment longer. He filled her with his masculine power, and she leashed it with her own femininity as she rode above him, setting the pace. They traveled through the realms of sensuality together, and their eyes locked, their souls met, at the critical juncture of total, exquisite satisfaction.

When Philip returned to the tower the following evening, he found Holly there as he'd hoped he would.

"I just stopped by to warm up the chicken for you," she said with a sheepish smile.

"I appreciate it, sweetheart." And he did, with all his heart. Whether Holly realized it or not, she had begun to share her life with him. Talk about a lucky break! Philip figured that by the time his cast was removed, she would be living with him on a permanent basis. "And since you're here, you might as well spend the night."

"Yes, I might as well." She simply couldn't stop herself from coming back to Philip each day. Her need to see him, hold him, care for him was greater than her fear of loving him too much.

They discussed their day apart during dinner. Philip had become familiar with the names and personalities of most of her students by now, and Holly understood the problems he was facing trying to get investors to back his latest building project.

"Ellis has agreed to design the condos," he told Holly. "He's the architect who asked me to come to Sweden last month. He believes in the concept as much as I do. He's seen it work in Europe successfully."

"Maybe you should have him talk to your board and key investors," Holly suggested.

"Great minds think alike," Philip said, smiling across the table at her. "He's coming to the States next week, and I'm going to give a big splashy party in his honor the Friday of Memorial Day weekend. I think you'll get a kick out of it, Holly."

"Me? I certainly won't be attending."

"But sweetheart, I'm going to need you there. I can't host a big party like that on my own while I'm on crutches." In truth, Philip could have made do without Holly, but he wanted to draw her out of her shell, out of her quiet, very private existence. It was an important part of the healing process, he figured. Besides, even a business party might be fun with Holly by his side.

"You must have plenty of qualified people on your staff to help you out."

"Yes, of course. And they'll be there. But you're the one I want as my hostess, Holly."

She stood and began clearing the table. "Well, I'm flattered, Philip. I really am. But I wouldn't feel comfortable around all those wealthy people. I don't come from that sort of background."

Philip laughed. "Neither do I. So what's the big deal? Just be yourself."

He always made everything sound so easy, Holly thought. "I wouldn't even know what to wear," she said.

"A dress," he supplied helpfully. "You know, one of those fancy dresses women wear to show off at big parties. With the sequins and ruffles and stuff."

"Oh, great. I have at least ten of them hanging in my closet," Holly said, loading the dishwasher. "I can wear my diamond tiara, too."

The next day Philip was waiting for Holly when she returned to his tower once again. "You're home early," she said, not even noticing how easily she referred to his place as home now.

"I'm going back to the office in a while. But first I wanted to see the fashion show."

She gave him a kiss, then patted King. "What are you talking about?"

"Let's go upstairs and find out."

The iron stairway leading to the bedroom was too narrow for Philip to get up with his crutches, but he and Holly had the routine down pat now. He handed them to her, hopped up using the rails for support, and she followed with them. At the top she handed him back his crutches.

"Good heavens, where'd all these clothes come from?" she asked when she saw an array of evening dresses in varied styles and hues draped across the bed.

"I called Bloomingdale's and had them delivered," Philip said. He pushed some aside and sat on the bed. "Why don't you try them on and see which ones you like best?"

"They're all so lovely. I wouldn't know where to start."

"How about that jazzy red number first? I've been picturing you in it all afternoon."

"It's a little too jazzy for my taste," she said, but she took off her simple gray dress and slipped on the flouncy piece of frippery to oblige him. "I wish you had a full-length mirror," she said.

"I didn't think of that. I'll have to be your mirror."

She twirled around for him, a little self-consciously. "Well?"

"It's great. Better than I imagined," he said. "Now try another."

She tried on an elegant pleated tea-length dress in ecru silk next, which was much more to her taste.

Philip applauded. "Love it. Demure yet sexy."

He also applauded a watercolor floral with a plunging sweetheart neckline, enthusiastically approved a gauzy gown of periwinkle blue and whistled his appreciation when she modeled a short black dress with a halter top.

"Philip, you're absolutely no help. You like everything."

"Because everything looks so good on you, sweetheart."

She glanced at the price tag of the dress she had on at the moment and whistled herself. "To think they can get away with asking so much for a couple yards of fabric and a designer's label. Ridiculous."

Philip shrugged. "The price doesn't matter. I want you to keep them all."

"Don't be absurd. I simply can't accept such an expensive—"

"Why not, dammit?"

His exasperation surprised her. She hadn't meant to offend him. "I appreciate your generosity," she said more graciously. "And I'll keep one dress to wear at your party." Until that moment she hadn't made up her mind that she was going to it. "Now help me decide which one."

"Oh, I'll leave that up to you," Philip said. His interest in fashion was limited to the pleasure it could give her. He only wished she'd let herself get carried away with it a little more, rather than hold back, limiting herself. He wondered if she were ever going to allow him to spoil her. He doubted it. It seemed so ironic to him that when he'd been poor he'd married a woman whose chief happiness in life was spending money. And now that he had more than enough, he loved a woman who couldn't have cared less. But it was more than the expense that stopped Holly, he knew. She was afraid to let herself be fully happy.

Holly sensed that she'd somehow disappointed him. "This was so sweet, so thoughtful of you," she told him and perched on his good leg like a delicate bird. She wrapped her arms around his neck and kissed him softly. "Do you have to go back to the office?"

"Absolutely," he replied sternly.

But Holly saw the glint in his eye and kissed him again, using the delicate persuasion of her lips and tongue in an eloquent plea for him to stay. "Do you *really* have to go back to the office?"

"Absolutely not!" he replied this time, falling back on the bed and pulling her down with him.

"Careful. We'll wrinkle the dresses, Philip."

"Good. Then you'll have to keep them all."

Holly decided to wear the ecru silk to Philip's party the following week. Its understated elegance appealed to her, and on a practical level, she appreciated the pocket hidden in the skirt pleats. She slipped the Goddess of Joy into it before leaving the tower and joining Philip in the main part of the mansion. She found him in the kitchen, conferring with the caterer. He seemed so at ease discussing caviar and smoked salmon, champagne and foie gras. Holly felt superfluous. She really had no place at this function, she told herself. She couldn't understand why Philip had wanted her to be a part of it. But when he turned to her with a smile, she basked in the warmth of it.

He was managing quite well with just a cane now, and after introducing Holly to the caterer, he took her arm and accompanied her to the drawing room. All the lamps were turned on, and there were flower arrangements in crystal vases everywhere. The French windows had been thrown open to let in the mild spring air. A bar had been set up in one corner, and the man tending it was diligently polishing glasses. Holly had the sense that the room itself was holding its breath, waiting for the party to begin.

Her mouth was dry, and she had difficulty swallowing. "The guests should be arriving any minute now," she said with a little hitch in her voice.

"No one ever arrives on time." Philip stepped back to take her in. "You look perfect," he pronounced.

She smoothed down the pleats in her dress with a damp palm. "I don't feel perfect. I feel stupid and nervous and completely out of my element," she blurted.

He took her icy hand. "I'll let you in on a little secret, Holly. So does everybody else a good part of the time."

"Not Philip Irons." How poised he looked in his formal wear, she thought. Even the fact that one trouser leg was split and his bulky cast bulged out of the side of it didn't ruin the elegant effect.

"Especially Philip Irons," he replied. "Sometimes, in the middle of one of my business parties, I wonder what the hell *I'm* doing at it. I have to stop myself from glancing over my shoulder to see if there's a bouncer heading my way to throw me out."

Holly smiled. "He'd have to be a pretty big bouncer to manage that."

"You bet." Philip stuck out his blunt chin. "I tussled with a few in my day. Of course that was before I got respectable." He twanged out the word. "The only thing I owned of any value then, aside from my carpentry tools, was a beautiful ivory netsuke. The one that happens to be in your pocket as we speak, sweetheart."

Holly's hand automatically slipped into her pocket to touch the goddess. "How did you know I had her with me?"

"Because you usually have her with you. Especially when you feel tense or nervous. The Goddess of Joy's become your talisman as she used to be mine."

"If she meant so much to you, why did you part with her, Philip?"

"For money." He could see how disappointed she was in his reply. "Sorry, but that's the truth, Holly. Like I said, the goddess was the only thing of value I owned. And I needed money to buy my future wife the diamond engagement ring she insisted on having. If I'd sold my tools, we would have starved to death."

Holly gazed up at him. "Then you gave me the wrong answer, darling. It was *love* that made you part with the goddess."

He shook his head. "Perhaps a close facsimile of it, anyway. At twenty a man can easily confuse lust with love."

"Men have been known to do that at thirty-eight, too."

"Not this one."

He bent and gave Holly a gentle kiss on the cheek. He knew what the genuine emotion felt like now. As wonderful as their lovemaking was, he knew his feelings for Holly ran so much deeper than sexual feelings. He couldn't wait for this party that hadn't even begun to be over. Once they were alone again in their tower retreat, he intended to ask Holly to marry him. He had it all planned out, down to the box containing the ring hidden under the sofa cushion.

The doorbell chimed, and he noticed how Holly's body tensed. "Don't worry, sweetheart. Just be yourself. It's going to be a piece of cake."

Holly's heart sank. She recalled that shortly after the last time Philip had uttered those exact words, he'd broken his leg. Now she feared that she was going to end up falling flat on her face.

Instead, she ended up surprising herself. Her experience conducting classes gave her a certain social ease. She remembered names and could ask the right questions to draw guests out while introducing them to each other. She also had a good understanding of Philip's latest project and made sure everyone met the guest of honor, the architect Elwood Ellis. She'd been most nervous about meeting him, aware of his world reputation and Philip's high regard for him. He turned out to be a warm, friendly man, and his wife, Martha, was just as charming and unassuming, with a dry wit that Holly found amusing.

By the end of the first hour, Holly actually found herself not only relaxing but having a good time. She smiled at Philip across the room, holding court on one of the sofas, his broken leg propped up on a leather hassock. Then she noticed new arrivals and hurried off to greet them. It was a wonderful party! she remarked to herself as she glided out to the foyer, the silk pleats of her dress softly swishing.

"Hello, I'm Holly Murphey," she said, extending her hand to the couple.

"Who?" the young woman asked, taking a step back.

The gray-haired man accompanying her accepted Holly's hand and gave it a brief, limp shake. "I'm Giles Grant, Ms. Murphey. And this is my daughter, Vivian."

What a beautiful young woman, Holly thought. "Welcome," she said. "Please let me introduce you to the guests of honor."

"But how silly," Vivian chirped. "Elwood and Martha are two of our dearest friends. I'm sure you're the only person here that we don't know, Ms. Murphey."

She brushed past Holly, her father in tow. Holly felt the chill as they passed, then did indeed feel rather silly, following their stiff backs into the drawing room. She saw them make a beeline for Philip. Vivian planted a kiss directly on Philip's lips, Holly noted.

"Ah, I see the Grants have arrived."

Holly turned to Martha Ellis and smiled with relief at the sight of the woman's congenial face. "Yes. I made the mistake of offering to introduce them to you. I didn't realize you were such close friends."

Martha raised an eyebrow. "Neither did I. Elwood designed their house in Palm Springs a few years ago, and their demands nearly drove him crazy. He's sworn off wasting his talents on the domiciles of the wealthy ever since." She took a dainty sip of champagne. "He simply doesn't have the kiss-ass personality for it, if you'll pardon my French."

"Pardon it? Are you kidding? I'll drink to it." Holly lifted a glass of champagne from the tray of a passing waiter and clicked it against Martha's. "Does Vivian usually attend parties with her father?"

"Oh, yes. They're very close. His wife died years ago, and Vivian is his only child. She'll inherit his entire fortune, of course. Giles is quite blatant about proclaiming that he'll give half of it over to her and the man she marries the moment they produce a grandchild. If you ask me, that's like asking every fortune hunter on the planet to come out of the woodwork."

"Poor Vivian," Holly said. "She'll never know if a man loves her for herself alone."

Martha chuckled. "Somehow I can't muster up too much sympathy for her." She plucked up an anchovy canapé from the silver tray of another passing waiter. "Vivian's been trained at Daddy's knee and knows how to pick a winner when she sees one."

Holly glanced over to Philip. "Poor Vivian" was sharing the hassock with his broken leg and stroking the plaster as if it were a piece of touchable art. "Like Philip Irons, you mean."

Martha popped the canapé into her mouth and chewed thoughtfully. "He *would* be the ideal catch for her. Inherited wealth always needs a healthy shot of the self-made man into the gene pool to keep it swimming along for a few more generations." She smiled at Holly. "But I think Philip has other ideas for his future. When he came to Sweden last month, he told us that he'd recently met someone very special. A woman whose description fits yours to a T, Holly."

"He hardly knew me then," Holly said.

"It doesn't take Philip long to make up his mind about people."

Holly's eyes wandered back to him. Something Vivian had just said seemed to amuse him tremendously.

"Don't worry about her," Martha said, following Holly's gaze. "It's quite obvious to me that she doesn't stand a chance now that you're in the picture, Holly."

Perhaps it's time I got out of the picture, Holly thought.

"The party was a triumph, King," Philip announced jubilantly when he and Holly returned to the tower in the early morning hours.

"Don't let him jump on your broken leg, Philip," Holly said testily, pulling King away.

"Well, he doesn't know it's broken, sweetheart."

"Then don't let him jump on you at all. Just look at your dinner jacket. It's covered with dog hairs." She brushed them off with rough swipes of her palm.

"I'm going to have to throw the suit out anyway, Holly. The pants are ruined, thanks to my cast."

She stopped swiping. "You must be exhausted, hobbling around all evening," she said. "That cane doesn't give you enough support. I think you stopped using crutches way too soon."

"Holly, I feel fine. And I didn't *hobble* around."

"That's right. You didn't. You sat around with Vivian Grant."

Philip laughed. "Is that why you're so grouchy now? Because you're jealous?"

"I'm neither. I'm just a little tired." She plopped down on the sofa and kicked off her high heels. "*I* didn't sit around all night with Vivian Grant." She began massaging her stockinged feet.

"That name does keep popping up, doesn't it?" Philip joined her, lifted her legs into his lap and took over the foot massage.

She sighed. "That feels heavenly."

"You were great tonight, Holly. The hostess with the mostest."

"I enjoyed it more than I expected I would. Do you think you'll get the support you need for your project now?"

"We'll see. Ellis certainly did his best to drum up enthusiasm. The trouble is, the project lacks glamour. It's too simple and straightforward. But dammit, Holly, I think it's a sound idea. The market's glutted with overpriced luxury condos now. Yet there's nothing available for people who need decent, affordable housing. It's crazy!"

"Ouch," she said. He'd practically twisted off her big toe in his enthusiasm.

"Sorry," he said, patting her foot. "I tend to get carried away on the subject." He wanted to direct the conversation to a subject of even more importance to him but felt uncharacteristically nervous about it. He delved his free hand under the sofa cushion and touched the ring box. He cleared his throat. "Why don't I open a bottle of champagne?"

Holly groaned. "I've had enough high living for one night. As soon as I can get up the energy to move, I'm going to heat up a pot of milk for us. Wouldn't you prefer a mug of warm milk, Philip?"

It wasn't exactly the romantic image he had in mind. Maybe it would be better to wait until tomorrow to ask her to marry him, Philip thought. But it went against his nature to procrastinate.

"She's really quite a lovely young woman," Holly said.

"What?" Philip frowned. "You're not talking about Vivian Grant again, are you, Holly? Forget about her. She's a spoiled little rich girl who means nothing to me and never will. I dated her a few times before I met you, and then I lost interest."

"Aha! So you *were* interested in her. And you probably still would be if you weren't involved with me."

"No way, Holly. You know who Vivian reminds me of? My ex-wife, that's who. Except that Caroline wasn't born into money. She expected me to make it for her. And God knows I did my best to give her everything she wanted. She wanted a ring, I gave her a ring. She wanted a house, I built her a house. She wanted a bigger house, I sold the first one for a profit and hired a few buddies to help me build her a bigger house." Philip laughed and shook his head. "That's how I got started in the contracting business. To please Caroline. But I couldn't make the money fast enough for her. Just when my business was finally taking off, she did, too."

"Where'd she go?"

"Straight into the arms of a fat, old man who happened to be very wealthy. He owned a fleet of fast-food franchises. You know what Caroline's parting words to me were?" Philip grinned. "She said that I would never amount to anything."

"So that's the secret of your success," Holly said. "You were spurred on to prove your ex-wife wrong."

"Sure, initially. But that was a long time ago. I haven't seen Caroline for over ten years, and I can barely remember what she looks like now. I worked hard, damn hard, just for the simple pleasure of it, and success kind of snowballed on me. But if I had to, I could give all this up and start over again without any regrets."

"You wouldn't regret giving up the mansion?" Holly nudged his side with her foot. "The limo? The hot-air balloon?"

"Well, maybe the balloon," he allowed. "And my netsuke collection. But that's it. If I can't get the investors I need for my project, I'm going to put up everything I own to back it myself. That's how sure I am of its success. But there *is* risk involved, a possibility that I may lose everything. I think you should know that, love, because I'm going to ask you..."

"Philip, let's not talk anymore," Holly interrupted. She'd suddenly sensed what he was leading up to. She flung her legs off his lap and stood abruptly. "It's almost dawn. I have to leave for Vermont in a few hours."

His eyes narrowed. "Since when are you going to Vermont?"

"Didn't I tell you? My mind's been on the party all week, and I must have forgotten." She was talking fast now. Very fast. "My brother invited me to spend Memorial Day weekend with him and his family. Maybe I should just change and leave now. It's a long drive." She turned and headed for the spiral staircase.

"Wait!" Philip commanded, pushing himself up. "Don't you dare run away from me now, Holly. You know what I was about to ask you, and I want your answer, dammit." He heard his own voice booming, and it echoed in his tightening heart. The tender marriage proposal he'd rehearsed in his mind all evening had come out an angry demand.

Holly paused, one foot on the first metal step. It felt cold beneath her bare sole, and she shivered. The time had come—the time to say goodbye to Philip. She'd resolved to do it after his cast had been removed, fooling herself into thinking that he needed her with him until then. But in truth her motive had been much more selfish. She'd wanted a few more precious weeks with him. She slowly turned to face him across the room.

"I'm not going to marry you, Philip."

His face paled, and he leaned on his cane for a moment, considering her statement. Then he straightened, his expression obstinate. "You will. Eventually."

She should have known he wouldn't accept what he didn't want to hear. Philip's biggest fault and strength was his stubborn determination to make life turn out the way he wanted it to. He was almost naive in his belief that whatever setbacks and losses he experienced could be overcome by his driving optimism—an optimism that she couldn't share with him.

"I've got to get out of your life so that you can get on with it, Philip," she told him softly, leaning against the stair rail for support. "You want a wife and family. You want someone to share your dreams and your future. You want all the things I can't give you."

"You give me exactly what I want, Holly," he replied, moving toward her. "You give me joy."

Her laugh was hollow, expressing all the hopelessness she felt at that moment. "Here's the only joy I can give you," she told him, digging into her pocket. She took out the Goddess of Joy and offered it to him. "Take it, Philip. I want you to have it as my parting gift to you."

He looked down at her trembling hand without moving.

"Take it!" she demanded.

"Sweetheart, you're tired," he said calmly. "You're not thinking clearly at the moment. Let's go to bed."

Oh, how she longed to do exactly that. How she wanted to lose herself in his warm embrace one more time. But she couldn't allow herself to be weak anymore. She clenched the netsuke in her fist.

"It's best that I leave right now," she said.

"You're not going anywhere, Holly." His voice remained calm, but anger flashed in his gray eyes like lightning. He wrapped his fingers around her arm, digging into silk fabric and soft flesh.

"Do you intend to keep me here by force?" Meeting his gaze, she faced him down, strong as a lightning rod.

He released her immediately, and she fled up the stairs to change into her jeans and sweater. When she came down again Philip was standing by the long arched window, watching the morning sky brighten. He didn't turn around when he heard her footsteps.

She had to fight down her compelling urge to rush to him, to wrap her arms around his waist and never let go. Instead, she headed for the door.

"I'm sorry I couldn't be the woman you wanted me to be, Philip," she told him in parting, praying he would turn to look at her.

But when he did his luminous gray eyes were so filled with pain that she wished he hadn't.

"I can't chase after you if you walk out on me now," he said, resting his weight on his cane. "Even if I could, I wouldn't, Holly. It seems as if you've left me so many times before, and I can't take it anymore. Every time you go you leave my soul hanging fire. Don't you realize that?"

The tears streamed down her face. "I'm sorry," she said again.

"I don't want your apologies!" he shouted. "I want your commitment to me!" He took a deep breath, and when he spoke again his voice was even. "Listen carefully, Holly. I don't want you ever coming back to me again unless it's to stay. Do you understand me?"

"Yes." The realization that she would never see him again hit her full force. She walked out while she still had the strength and will. She left without even kissing him goodbye. She softly closed the door behind her.

King trotted to the door and scratched at it, whining.

"Don't worry, pal. She'll be back. For good."

And Philip clung to that belief until he went upstairs and saw the Goddess of Joy lying on his pillow. He picked it up and held it in his palm. It meant nothing to him now. He wondered how Holly could have been so heartless as to take his joy from him and leave him nothing but an ivory figure to replace it.

Chapter Thirteen

When Holly pulled up in front of her brother's rambling farmhouse five hours later, she was numb with exhaustion, drained of emotion. She'd called her brother from her apartment and asked him if she could visit for the weekend. He'd assured her that she would be more than welcome. He came out of the house to greet her now, a stocky man with gray at the temples of his dark brown hair. He was followed by a big, homely mutt. The moment Holly stepped out of the car, the dog bounded forward.

"Lucky!" she cried, crouching to press her face against his. The she stood and hugged her brother. She hadn't seen him since the Easter holidays.

"Thanks for letting me come visit on such short notice, Paul. I just had this impulse to visit you and the family."

"We're glad you did. Joan and the girls are shopping in Arlington now. They'll be back for lunch." He stepped away to study Holly. His eyes were the same brilliant blue as hers. "What's wrong, Sis? You look terrible."

"I don't want to talk about it now, okay?"

"Okay." He ruffled her hair. "But you really do look beat. Why don't you go take a nap before your rambunctious nieces come home?"

"That's a brilliant suggestion."

"Could you expect anything less from your big brother? Go right upstairs. The guest room's all made up for you. I'll bring up your suitcase."

"Thanks. It's in the trunk." Holly handed him her car keys.

She'd already turned down the quilt, taken off her shoes and thrown herself on the bed when Paul came into the room with a big cardboard box in his arms.

"Oh, you didn't have to bring up that box, Paul. It's been sitting in the car for weeks, since Grace handed it over to me. Mom gave it to her before she moved to Florida."

"Holly's High School Mementos," he read. "Want me to take it back down?"

"No, leave it up here. The girls might enjoy looking through it later. I think my old cheerleader uniform's in there."

Her brother put it down and sat at the edge of the bed. "You were the best cheerleader in the history of Central High, Sis."

"Not that you're prejudiced or anything."

"Maybe I am, but you really were, Holly. You know what made you so great? You had such exuberance, such high spirits. It was like you had this contagious joy in you that spread to the grandstands."

"I was nothing special, Paul."

"You were, Holly. You *are*. I hate to see you so sad again." He took her hand and patted it. "After your visit last Easter, Joan and I remarked how well you seemed to be doing. More like the old Holly you were before... well, before the accident."

"That Holly doesn't exist anymore." She closed her eyes for just a moment.

But when she opened them again, Paul was gone and the room was dusky. She lifted her arm and squinted at her watch. It was past six o'clock. And then she sensed the presence of someone watching her every move. She heard panting. She sat up quickly and looked across the room. Two pairs of eyes stared at her from just inside the doorway. Lucky's big brown ones. And her youngest niece Jody's bright blue ones.

"You're up at last, Aunt Holly!"

Without waiting for an invitation, since she knew one wasn't needed, the little girl ran across the room and jumped into bed with Holly. So did Lucky.

"Will you open up that box now?" Jody demanded after hugs and kisses. "Daddy said you had a costume in it that you'd let us try on."

"A uniform, honey. It's nothing fancy."

"Come on, Aunt Holly," Jody said, tugging her hand. "Let's see it. I've been waiting for you to wake up for over a hundred hours."

"Wow, I guess I did sleep a long time." Getting out of bed to do Jody's bidding, Holly turned on a lamp and tore open the box.

"There's just a bunch of old stuff in here, honey," she said, glad to have her little niece's company as she sifted through it. She doubted she would have gotten up the nerve to open the box alone. "Here's the uniform you wanted to see." Holly shook out the folds of the green sweater with a big gold C sewn on the front and a gold-and-white pleated skirt.

"Oh." Jody's expectant face dropped.

Holly laughed. "I told you it was nothing fancy." Still, she lovingly smoothed out the wrinkles, remembering how Daniel's eyes glowed with pride when she wore it.

"Yuck, what's this?" Jody asked, taking out a plastic box with something brown and shriveled inside.

"That, dear girl, was my first corsage."

Jody still looked puzzled.

"It's all dried out now, but it was once a beautiful orchid." She remembered Daniel nervously pinning it to her gown, stabbing her with the pin.

Jody flipped through her high-school yearbook, then put it aside, uninterested. Holly sat on the floor and opened a pink plastic photo album. Jody leaned over her shoulder, resting her sharp little chin on it, to look at the pictures with her. Holly inhaled her scent, a mixture of bubble gum and bubble bath.

"Here's me in my uniform," Holly said.

"Who's that guy with you?"

"Daniel. We were going steady then. See?" Holly pointed to the ring dangling from a gold chain around her neck. "That was *his* ring. I married him. He died when you were only two, Jody, so you probably don't remember him."

"He drowned with your little boy, right? My cousin Danny."

"Yes, that's right. They died together."

"Do you have any pictures of Danny in there?"

"No. These pictures were taken long before he was born." She turned the page. "Look, here's your dad."

"That's Daddy?" Jody gave a screech that vibrated through Holly's eardrum. "Is he wearing a Halloween costume? Is that a wig and false beard?"

Holly chuckled. "No, dear. That's the way he looked for real in those days, much to your grandmother's chagrin. Your dad was a hippie."

"And proud of it," Paul said from the doorway.

"Daddy, you looked so funny!"

"Didn't I tell you not to disturb Aunt Holly?"

"She didn't, Paul. Why'd you let me sleep so late?"

"Because you obviously needed it. Joan sent me up to ask if you'd be ready for dinner around seven."

"Sure. I'll just freshen up."

"Jody, go tell Mom that Aunt Holly is going to have dinner with us, okay?" When the little girl ran off Paul offered his hand and pulled Holly to her feet. "I overheard you talking about Daniel and Danny. I hope Jody's questions didn't upset you."

"No. I didn't find it upsetting at all to talk about them. For the first time I truly felt I could deal with their deaths." And a comforting peace suffused Holly as she stated this.

Early the next morning Holly took a long walk in the woods behind her brother's house, accompanied by Lucky. The dog hadn't let her out of his sight since she'd arrived.

Spring's bounty was in full flourish, glowing in the golden light, and dewdrops shimmered on the wildflowers as chickadees and warblers twittered in the budding dogwoods and maples. But Holly saw and heard none of this. She was thinking about Philip. She longed for him and knew that he was longing for her, too. She could feel his heart pulling at hers, pulling her back to him.

She loved him. That's all she knew for sure. She smiled, remembering his antics at the bowling alley to entertain Snake. Their little *baku*. Holly sighed. Their little boy for less than twenty-four hours.

She leaned against a red maple and lifted her face to the sun. Staring at the branches above, she noticed that new leaves were beginning to burst out of the scarlet buds. She looked around her and saw everything surging to life after a period of dormancy, proof of nature's indomitable force. The trilliums bloomed again, the jacks-in-the-pulpit had popped through the once frozen ground, ferns unfurled as if stretching after a long, deep nourishing sleep.

Holly could feel that same life force surging through her bloodstream. She felt the healing power of it, the healing that had been slowing restoring her.

In a flash of enlightenment she understood that she was able to love Philip so completely because the time had come for her to awaken to life after her own long dormancy. She was ready once again to face its challenges instead of fearing them. She could never be the same carefree person she once was. She'd taken life for granted before and accepted happiness as her due. She'd thought she was invulnerable. But now she had to accept the hard truth that there were no guarantees against losing what was most precious to her. She had to accept and go on. She couldn't deny the past, but she couldn't refuse to embrace the future, either. Yes, she'd experienced the ultimate loss of a child. And she'd almost died from the all-encompassing grief. But she'd survived. She'd *survived*!

Struck by the power of her own resilience—the resilience of the human spirit—she flung her arms wide in joy.

Philip heard her light footsteps coming up the stone tower steps even before King did. But he didn't move. He continued reading the real-estate section of the Sunday paper that was spread out before him on the kitchen table. Rather, he pretended to read as the words blurred in front of his eyes. He didn't look up when she entered and wished King didn't make such a big show of greeting her. He certainly wasn't going to.

"Hello, darling. I'm home," she said. "For good this time."

That's all it took for Philip to give up his act of indifference. He stood up so quickly the chair toppled over. "Well, it's about time," he said, attempting to look fierce. He hoped she didn't notice the tears of relief in his eyes.

She did. But she didn't let on. She hurried across the room to embrace him. "I was thinking on the drive from Vermont that I'd like a big wedding, Philip. A huge celebration. Would that be all right with you?"

"Yes, I'd like—" His voice broke and he cleared his throat. "I'd like that, too, sweetheart."

"Good. I've got an idea for the reception that I think you'll like, too."

"Tell me about it." But before she could, his lips covered hers in an all-consuming kiss that expressed all the love and passion and need for her that he'd been unable to utter since she'd returned to him. "Tell me about it in bed," he said.

Holly happily led the way up the spiral staircase. She had more than just wedding plans to discuss with him. She moved to his netsuke display case and opened it. "Can I take back my Goddess of Joy?" she asked sweetly.

He laughed. "Why, you little Indian giver."

She snatched it up and rubbed it between her palms. "Well, I don't *really* believe it has magical powers, but it brought us together, and I'd like it to bring us some more good luck now." She looked at Philip, the glow of love lighting her face. "I want to get pregnant, darling."

Again the tears of relief sprang to his eyes, and this time he didn't care if she saw them.

On a bright, vividly clear day in July, Holly and Philip held their wedding reception in the open field that would soon be the condominium village Philip had been dreaming about. As soon as he'd made it known that he was putting up all his own money to build it, investors begged to be included in the venture.

Two large striped tents were set up on the field, one housing a band and dance floor, the other a huge buffet table that Mike Murphey took great delight in. All the Murpheys attended Holly's wedding, and so did all her students. Mr. Brakenbiddle escorted Lady Gladys to it.

And toward the end of the festivities, when the wind picked up, Holly and Philip made their getaway in their big balloon. They waved to the cheering crowd below, and Holly tossed her bouquet. Vivian Grant caught it.

Holly piloted the balloon, stair-stepping higher and higher and locating an air mass moving in the desired direction quite smartly. Next to the wedding ceremony, it was the highlight of her day.

"I have something to tell you, Philip," she announced after they'd floated along for awhile. "Let me whisper it in your ear."

"Sweetheart, no one can overhear but the birds."

"Well, it's something that concerns the birds." She paused. "And the bees."

He grinned and took her into his arms. "Oh, Holly, that's wonderful news. The best wedding present you could possibly give me."

"If it's a girl I'd like to name her Joy."

"And if it's a boy?"

"Oh, I don't know. I'm kind of partial to Snake."

* * * * *

INDULGE A LITTLE SWEEPSTAKES

OFFICIAL RULES

SWEEPSTAKES RULES AND REGULATIONS. NO PURCHASE NECESSARY.

1. NO PURCHASE NECESSARY. To enter complete the official entry form and return with the invoice in the envelope provided. Or you may enter by printing your name, complete address and your daytime phone number on a 3 x 5 piece of paper. Include with your entry the hand printed words "Indulge A Little Sweepstakes." Mail your entry to: Indulge A Little Sweepstakes, P.O. Box 1397, Buffalo, NY 14269-1397. No mechanically reproduced entries accepted. Not responsible for late, lost, misdirected mail, or printing errors.

2. Three winners, one per month (Sept. 30, 1989, October 31, 1989 and November 30, 1989), will be selected in random drawings. All entries received prior to the drawing date will be eligible for that month's prize. This sweepstakes is under the supervision of MARDEN-KANE, INC. an independent judging organization whose decisions are final and binding. Winners will be notified by telephone and may be required to execute an affidavit of eligibility and release which must be returned within 14 days, or an alternate winner will be selected.

3. Prizes: 1st Grand Prize (1) a trip for two to Disneyworld in Orlando, Florida. Trip includes round trip air transportation, hotel accommodations for seven days and six nights, plus up to $700 expense money (ARV $3,500). 2nd Grand Prize (1) a seven-night Chandris Caribbean Cruise for two includes transportation from nearest major airport, accommodations, meals plus up to $1,000 in expense money (ARV $4,300). 3rd Grand Prize (1) a ten-day Hawaiian holiday for two includes round trip air transportation for two, hotel accommodations, sightseeing, plus up to $1,200 in spending money (ARV $7,700). All trips subject to availability and must be taken as outlined on the entry form.

4. Sweepstakes open to residents of the U.S. and Canada 18 years or older except employees and the families of Torstar Corp., its affiliates, subsidiaries and Marden-Kane, Inc. and all other agencies and persons connected with conducting this sweepstakes. All Federal, State and local laws and regulations apply. Void wherever prohibited or restricted by law. Taxes, if any are the sole responsibility of the prize winners. Canadian winners will be required to answer a skill testing question. Winners consent to the use of their name, photograph and/or likeness for publicity purposes without additional compensation.

5. For a list of prize winners, send a stamped, self-addressed envelope to Indulge A Little Sweepstakes Winners, P.O. Box 701, Sayreville, NJ 08871.

DL-SWPS

INDULGE A LITTLE SWEEPSTAKES

OFFICIAL RULES

SWEEPSTAKES RULES AND REGULATIONS. NO PURCHASE NECESSARY.

1. NO PURCHASE NECESSARY. To enter complete the official entry form and return with the invoice in the envelope provided. Or you may enter by printing your name, complete address and your daytime phone number on a 3 x 5 piece of paper. Include with your entry the hand printed words "Indulge A Little Sweepstakes." Mail your entry to: Indulge A Little Sweepstakes, P.O. Box 1397, Buffalo, NY 14269-1397. No mechanically reproduced entries accepted. Not responsible for late, lost, misdirected mail, or printing errors.

2. Three winners, one per month (Sept. 30, 1989, October 31, 1989 and November 30, 1989), will be selected in random drawings. All entries received prior to the drawing date will be eligible for that month's prize. This sweepstakes is under the supervision of MARDEN-KANE, INC. an independent judging organization whose decisions are final and binding. Winners will be notified by telephone and may be required to execute an affidavit of eligibility and release which must be returned within 14 days, or an alternate winner will be selected.

3. Prizes: 1st Grand Prize (1) a trip for two to Disneyworld in Orlando, Florida. Trip includes round trip air transportation, hotel accommodations for seven days and six nights, plus up to $700 expense money (ARV $3,500). 2nd Grand Prize (1) a seven-night Chandris Caribbean Cruise for two includes transportation from nearest major airport, accommodations, meals plus up to $1,000 in expense money (ARV $4,300). 3rd Grand Prize (1) a ten-day Hawaiian holiday for two includes round trip air transportation for two, hotel accommodations, sightseeing, plus up to $1,200 in spending money (ARV $7,700). All trips subject to availability and must be taken as outlined on the entry form.

4. Sweepstakes open to residents of the U.S. and Canada 18 years or older except employees and the families of Torstar Corp., its affiliates, subsidiaries and Marden-Kane, Inc. and all other agencies and persons connected with conducting this sweepstakes. All Federal, State and local laws and regulations apply. Void wherever prohibited or restricted by law. Taxes, if any are the sole responsibility of the prize winners. Canadian winners will be required to answer a skill testing question. Winners consent to the use of their name, photograph and/or likeness for publicity purposes without additional compensation

5. For a list of prize winners, send a stamped, self-addressed envelope to Indulge A Little Sweepstakes Winners, P.O. Box 701, Sayreville, NJ 08871.

© 1989 HARLEQUIN ENTERPRISES LTD.

DL-SWPS

INDULGE A LITTLE—WIN A LOT!

Summer of '89 Subscribers-Only Sweepstakes

OFFICIAL ENTRY FORM

This entry must be received by: October 31, 1989
This month's winner will be notified by: Nov. 7, 1989
Trip must be taken between: Dec. 7, 1989–April 7, 1990
(depending on sailing schedule)

YES, I want to win the Caribbean cruise vacation for two! I understand the prize includes round-trip airfare, a one-week cruise including private cabin and all meals, and a daily allowance as revealed on the "Wallet" scratch-off card.

Name ______________________________

Address ______________________________

City ____________ State/Prov. ______ Zip/Postal Code ______

Daytime phone number ______________________________
Area code

Return entries with invoice in envelope provided. Each book in this shipment has two entry coupons — and the more coupons you enter, the better your chances of winning!

DINDL-2

INDULGE A LITTLE—WIN A LOT!

Summer of '89 Subscribers-Only Sweepstakes

OFFICIAL ENTRY FORM

This entry must be received by: October 31, 1989
This month's winner will be notified by: Nov. 7, 1989
Trip must be taken between: Dec. 7, 1989–April 7, 1990
(depending on sailing schedule)

YES, I want to win the Caribbean cruise vacation for two! I understand the prize includes round-trip airfare, a one-week cruise including private cabin and all meals, and a daily allowance as revealed on the "Wallet" scratch-off card.

Name ______________________________

Address ______________________________

City ____________ State/Prov. ______ Zip/Postal Code ______

Daytime phone number ______________________________
Area code

Return entries with invoice in envelope provided. Each book in this shipment has two entry coupons — and the more coupons you enter, the better your chances of winning!

© 1989 HARLEQUIN ENTERPRISES LTD.

DINDL-2